Edge of Armageddon

(Matt Drake #13)

By

David Leadbeater

Thriller, adventure, action, mystery, suspense, archaeological,
military, historical

Other Books by David Leadbeater:

The Matt Drake Series
The Bones of Odin (Matt Drake #1)
The Blood King Conspiracy (Matt Drake #2)
The Gates of hell (Matt Drake 3)
The Tomb of the Gods (Matt Drake #4)
Brothers in Arms (Matt Drake #5)
The Swords of Babylon (Matt Drake #6)
Blood Vengeance (Matt Drake #7)
Last Man Standing (Matt Drake #8)
The Plagues of Pandora (Matt Drake #9)
The Lost Kingdom (Matt Drake #10)
The Ghost Ships of Arizona (Matt Drake #11)
The Last Bazaar (Matt Drake #12)

The Alicia Myles Series
Aztec Gold (Alicia Myles #1)
Crusader's Gold (Alicia Myles #2)

The Disavowed Series:
The Razor's Edge (Disavowed #1)
In Harm's Way (Disavowed #2)
Threat Level: Red (Disavowed #3)

The Chosen Few Series
Chosen (The Chosen Trilogy #1)
Guardians (The Chosen Tribology #2)

Short Stories
Walking with Ghosts (A short story)
A Whispering of Ghosts (A short story)

Connect with the author on Twitter: @dleadbeater2011
Visit the author's website: **www.davidleadbeater.com**

All helpful, genuine comments are welcome. I would love to hear from you.
davidleadbeater2011@hotmail.co.uk

CHAPTER ONE

Julian Marsh had always been a man of contrasting colors. One side black, the other gray . . . to infinity. Oddly, he never showed any interest as to why he evolved a little differently to the rest, merely accepted it, learned to live with it, reveled in it. To all intents and purposes it made him an object of interest; it diverted attention from the machinations going on behind the distinctive eyes and the salt-and-pepper hair. Marsh was always going to be outstanding—one way or another.

Inside, he was a different person again. Inner focus centered his attention to a single nucleus. For this month it was the cause of the Pythians, or rather what was left of them. The odd group had attracted his attention and then just dissolved around him. Tyler Webb was more a psychopathic mega-stalker than a cabalistic leader. But Marsh enjoyed the opportunity of departing alone, of masterminding a personal, eccentric design. To hell with Zoe Sheers and whomever else remained operational inside the sect, and to an even deeper hell with Nicholas Bell. Strapped, cuffed and waterboarded, no doubt the ex-builder would be spilling all to the authorities to gain even the slightest reprieve.

For Marsh, the future looked bright, if a little

tinged. There were two sides to every story and he was very much the two-sided man. After a regretful departure from Ramses' ill-fated bazaar—the pavilions with all their offerings appealed so very much—Marsh took to the skies with the help of an abyss-black helicopter. Swooping away he quickly turned his mind to the new adventure at hand.

New York.

Marsh checked the device at his side, moving it closer, unsure as to what he was seeing but confident about what it could do. This baby was the ultimate bargaining tool. The Big Daddy of absolute persuasion. Who could argue with a nuclear bomb? Marsh left the device well alone, checking over the outer pack and loosening the shoulder straps to accommodate his hefty frame. Of course, he would have to subject the thing to tests and verify its authenticity. After all, most bombs could be prepared to look like something they weren't—if the cook was good enough. Only then would the White House bow.

Risky, risky, one side of him said.

But fun! the other insisted. And worth a little radiation poisoning if it came to that.

Marsh laughed at himself. Such a rogue. But the mini Geiger-counter he'd brought along remained silent, feeding his bravado.

Being totally honest though, flying was not his thing. Yes, there was the exhilaration but there was also the chance of hot death—and right now that really didn't appeal to him. Perhaps another time. Marsh had spent many agonizing hours planning this mission, ensuring every waypoint was in place and as reasonably safe as could be, though considering the places he would be stopping off, that notion was almost laughable.

Take right now, for instance. They were headed over the canopy above the Amazon rainforest on the way to Columbia. A man waited for him there—more than one, in fact, and Marsh had imprinted his personality on the meet by insisting they wear white. Just a small concession, but an important one to the Pythian.

Is that all I am now?

Marsh laughed aloud, causing the pilot of the chopper to glance around in alarm.

"Everything okay?" the scarred, skinny man asked.

"Well, that depends on your point of view." Marsh laughed. "And how many points of view you have. I prefer to entertain more than one. You?"

The pilot turned away, grunting something unintelligible. Marsh shook his head. If only the unwashed masses knew the forces that crept and sneaked and undulated beneath them, never caring or considering the chaos they caused.

Marsh watched the landscape below, wondering for the millionth time if this point of entry into the US was the right way to go. When it came down to it, there were only two real options—through Canada or through Mexico. The latter country was closer to the Amazon and riddled with corruption; chock-full of men who could be paid to help and keep their mouths shut. Canada offered a few safe havens for men like

3

Marsh, but not enough and nowhere near the variety present in South America. As the monotonous landscape continued to unfold below, Marsh found his mind wandering.

The boy had grown up privileged with something far beyond a silver spoon in his mouth; more a solid gold ingot. The best schools and the best teachers—read "best" as "most expensive", Marsh always amended—tried to straighten him out, but failed. Maybe a stint in some kind of normalized school would have helped, but his parents were wealthy pillars of southern society and far out of touch with reality. Marsh was raised by servants and saw his parents mostly at meal times and luxurious functions, where he was ordered not to speak. Always the critical eye from his father, ensuring immaculate behavior. And always the guilty smile from his mother, knowing that her son was growing up loveless and alone but quite unable to bring herself to raise any form of challenge. And so Julian Marsh grew, developed and turned into what his father openly described as "an odd boy".

The pilot spoke and Marsh completely missed it. "Say again?"

"We are approaching Cali, sir. Columbia."

Marsh leaned over and watched a new scene unfold below. Cali was known as one of the most violent cities in the Americas and the home of the Cali Cartel—one of the world's biggest cocaine suppliers. On any normal day a man like Marsh took his life in his hands walking the byways of the El Calvario neighborhood, where rag-and-bone men combed the streets for garbage and slept in flophouses, where locals suffered the label of "tolerance zone", enabling commercial drug use and sex to flourish with minimal police mediation.

Marsh knew this was the place for him and his nuke.

Setting down, the pilot showed Marsh to a gray pickup truck, wherein sat three bulky men with cold, dead eyes and expressionless faces. Openly carrying firearms, they ushered Marsh into the truck, offering only a brief greeting. Then they were driving through the damp, cluttered streets, filthy buildings and rusted overhangs, offering his well-traveled eye yet another alternate view of the world, of a place where a chunk of the population "floated" from one hovel to the next, having no permanent home. Marsh withdrew a little, knowing he had little say over what happened next. These stops were necessary though if he were to successfully smuggle the nuke into the US, and worth any risk. And of course Marsh appeared as neutral as he could, keeping a few tricks up his multi-colored sleeves.

The vehicle meandered its way up into some mist-covered, rolling hills, eventually pulling into a paved driveway that fronted a large, quiet house. The journey had been made in silence but now one of the guards turned an inflexible countenance upon Marsh.

"We are here."

"Evidently. But where is here?"

Not too disrespectful. Not too whiny. Keep it all together.

"Bring your backpack." The guard jumped out and

opened the door. "Mr. Navarro is awaiting you."

Marsh nodded. It was the correct name and the correct place. He wouldn't be staying here for long, just enough time to make sure his next mode of transport and its final destination was unhampered and secure. He followed the guard under a low hanging arch replete with dripping droplets of mist and then into the dark entranceway of the old house. No lights shone inside and the appearance of an old ghost or two would be neither a surprise nor a worry. Marsh often saw and conversed with old specters in the dark.

The guard indicated an opening on the right. "You paid for a private room to yourself for a maximum of four hours. Go right on in."

Marsh inclined his head in thanks and pushed at the heavy door. "I also asked for permission to land an onward mode of transport. A chopper?"

"Yes. That is good too. Call me on the intercom when it is time and I will escort you through the house."

Marsh nodded in satisfaction. The money he had paid, over and above what was required, should ensure the best service and, so far, it had. Of course paying beyond the asking price also aroused suspicion, but those were the risks.

Two sides again, he thought. *Ying and yang. Marsh and Marsh. Black and . . . black with crimson bolts flashed through . . .*

Inside, the room was sumptuous. A corner sofa occupied the far side, made of black leather and deeply plush. A glass table with drinks decanter, wine and spirits stood nearby whilst a pod-machine offered coffee and tea in another corner. Snacks lay out on the glass table. Marsh smiled at it all.

Comfortable, but only for a short time. Perfect.

He slid in a pod of the strongest coffee and took a moment waiting for it to brew. Then he settled into the sofa and withdrew a laptop, placing the backpack carefully on the deep leather by his side. *Never has a nuclear bomb been so pampered,* he thought, wondering for a moment if he should prepare it a brew of its own. Of course, to a man like Marsh that was a no-brainer and within minutes the backpack sat with a steaming cup and a small iced cupcake at its side.

Marsh smiled. All was well.

A stint on the Internet; confirming emails told him that the onward chopper was already entering Columbia. No flags had been raised anywhere as yet, but it was still only hours since he left the bazaar in full swing. Marsh drank up and packed a small sandwich bag for the next flight, then buzzed the intercom.

"I am ready to leave."

Twenty minutes later and he was in the air again, the flight of the backpack-nuke a twisted but comfortable one. They were aiming for Panama, where he would end the quick flights and begin the tiresome leg of his journey along the ground. The pilot veered his way through the air and through any patrols, the best at what he did and handsomely paid.

When Panama's sprawl began to appear out of the left-hand window, Marsh began to realize how much closer he already was to the United States of America.

Hurricane's a-coming guys, and it ain't gonna pass easy . . .

He settled in Panama City for several hours, changing twice and showering four times, each with a different scented shampoo. The scents mingled nicely and scraped away the faint aroma of sweat. He ate breakfast and lunch even though it was dinner-time, and partook of three glasses of wine, each from a different bottle and colors. Life was good. The view outside the window didn't change and didn't inspire, so Marsh fished out a case of lipstick he saved for just such an occasion and colored the pane bright red. That helped, at least for a little while. Marsh then began to envision what it would be like to lick that pane clean, but at that moment the ping of an incoming message interrupted his daydreams.

ETA—15 minutes.

Marsh grimaced, happy but dismayed at the same time. A forty-hour road journey lay ahead, along some of the worst roads in the region. Not a thought likely to inspire. Still, once done the next stage would be infinitely more interesting. Marsh packed up, arranged the coffee pods, wine bottles and utensils in order of color, shape and size and then headed out.

The SUV was waiting, burbling at the curb, and looking surprisingly comfortable. Marsh arranged the nuke, wrapped a seatbelt around it, and then attended to himself. The driver chatted for a while before realizing that Marsh couldn't care less about his own shitty little life, and then settled down to drive. The road stretched interminably ahead.

Hours passed. The SUV glided and then jounced and then glided again, stopping several times for gas and spot checks. The driver wouldn't risk being pulled over for a misdemeanor. In the end, this was just one more vehicle among many, one more spark of life traveling the eternal highway to destinations unknown, and if it stayed unremarkable it would pass unnoticed.

And then Monterrey lay ahead. Marsh began to smile hugely, tired but pleased, the long journey over halfway gone.

The suitcase nuke sat beside him, now only a matter of hours from the US border.

CHAPTER TWO

Marsh made the next leg of his journey under cover of total darkness. This was where everything would be won or lost; the unknown factor being raised an inestimable amount by local cartel bosses being introduced to the mix. Who could guess the minds of such people? Who knew what they would do next?

Certainly not them . . . or Julian Marsh. He was transported ignominiously, along with a dozen other people, in the rear of a truck bound for the border. Somewhere along the way this truck veered off the track and vanished into the blackness. No lights, no guides, the driver knew this route blindfolded—and it was good that he did.

Marsh remained aloof in the back of the truck, listening to families prattle and fret. The scope of his plan loomed before him. The moment of his New York arrival couldn't come soon enough. When the truck ground to a halt and the rear doors swung open on oiled hinges he was the first out, seeking the leader of the armed men who stood watch.

"Diablo," he said, using the code word that identified him as a VIP traveler, and that he had agreed upon payment. The man nodded but then ignored him, herding everyone into a small huddle beneath the widespread branches of an overhanging tree.

"It is vital now," he said in Spanish, "that you move quietly, say nothing, and do as you are told. If you do not I will slit your throat. Do you understand?" Marsh watched as the man met every eye including his own. The march began a moment later, along a rutted track and through stands of trees. Moonlight flittered up above, and the lead Mexican often waited until clouds obscured the brightness before continuing. Very few words were passed, and those only by the men with guns, but suddenly Marsh found himself wishing that he spoke a little Spanish—or a lot, perhaps.

He trudged in the middle of the line, ignoring the frightened faces all around. After an hour they slowed and Marsh saw a rolling, sandy plain ahead, dotted by straggles of trees, cacti and little else. The entire group crouched down.

"Good so far," the leader whispered. "But now is the hard part. Border Patrol cannot watch the entire boundary constantly but they make spot checks. All the time. And you—" he nodded at Marsh "—have requested the Diablo crossing. I hope you are ready for it."

Marsh grunted. He had no idea what the little guy was talking about. Soon though, men started disappearing, each with a small group of immigrants, until only Marsh, the leader, and one guard were left.

"I am Gomez," the leader said. "This is Lopez. We will see you safely through the tunnel."

"And those guys?" Marsh nodded at the departed immigrants, effecting a fake American accent as best he could.

"They pay only five thousand per head." Gomez made a dismissive gesture. "They take their chances with the bullets. Do not worry, you can trust us."

Marsh started at the sly smile fixed firmly upon his guide's face. Of course, the entire journey had progressed far too smoothly to expect it to continue. The question was—when would they jump him?

"Let's get into the tunnel," he said. "I can feel prying eyes out here."

Gomez couldn't stop a flash of worry flickering across his face and Lopez scanned the darkness all around. As one the two men ushered him in an easterly direction, at a slight angle but toward the border. Marsh blundered along, deliberately misstepping and appearing inadequate. At one point Lopez even reached out to help him along, a helping hand which Marsh catalogued for later, logging it as a weakness. He was by no means an expert, but a bottomless bank account had once afforded him many things beside material trappings, the experience of world champion martial artists and ex-Special Forces troops among them. Marsh knew a few tricks, rusty though he may be.

They walked for a while, the desert stretching out around them and almost soundless. When a rolling hill appeared ahead, Marsh was fully prepared to start climbing, but Gomez stopped and pointed out a feature he otherwise would never have seen. Where the sandy ground met the sloping foothills a pair of small trees met a tangle of brush. It wasn't toward this arrangement that Gomez walked, however, it was a careful thirty paces to the right and then ten more up the steepest slope. Once there Lopez scanned the area with infinite care.

"Clear," he said at length.

Gomez then scrabbled around for a length of buried rope and began to pull. Marsh saw a small section of the hillside rise up, displacing stones and brush to reveal a man-size hole that had been hewn out of the living stone. Gomez slipped inside and then Lopez waved the barrel of his gun at Marsh.

"You now. You too."

Marsh followed, ducking his head carefully and watching for the trap he knew was only moments away from being sprung. Then, as an after-thought, the man with two sides switched channels, deciding to inch back out into the darkness.

Lopez was waiting, gun up. Marsh slipped, boots scrabbling down the stony slope. Lopez reached out, weapon dropping, and Marsh brought a six-inch blade swinging around, burying its point in the other man's carotid. Lopez's eyes went wide, and a hand came up to staunch the flow, but Marsh was having none of it. He punched Lopez between the eyes, wrestled his gun free and then kicked the dying body down the slope.

Fuck you.

Marsh dropped the rifle, knowing Gomez would catch on quicker than necessary if he saw it in Marsh's hand. Then he re-entered the tunnel and quickly made his way down the initial passage. It was rough and ready, held up by shaking timbers, dust and mortar dribbling down from the roof. Marsh fully expected to be buried at any moment. Gomez's voice reached his straining ears.

"Don't worry. That is just the false entry to scare any who might stumble upon this tunnel. Come further down, my friend."

Marsh knew exactly what would be waiting for him "further down", but he did now have a small element of surprise. The tricky part would be disabling Gomez's weapon without sustaining a nasty wound. New York was still thousands of miles away.

And it seemed much further, stood as he was under the Mexican desert, feeling the drip-drip of dirt down his back, and surrounded by the stench of sweat and vegetation, his eyes stung by dust.

Marsh ventured forward, crawling at one point and dragging the backpack behind, a strap looped around his ankle. It's full of clothes, he thought at one point. Just clothes and maybe a toothbrush. A nice cologne. A sachet of coffee . . . he wondered where the Americans might station their radiation sensing devices, then began to worry about the radiation itself. Again.

Probably something you should have checked before setting off.

Ah, well, you live and learn.

Marsh made himself laugh just as he emerged from the narrow tunnel and into a much larger one. Gomez was bending down, holding a hand out to help.

"Something funny?"

"Yeah, your fucking teeth."

Gomez stared, shocked and disbelieving. That

sentence it seemed, was the last thing he expected to hear at this point in their journey. Marsh had calculated that it might be. As Gomez tried to compute, Marsh rose, twisted the gun in Gomez's hands, and rammed the butt into the other man's mouth.

"Now do you see what I mean?"

Gomez wrestled hard, pushing Marsh away and bringing the barrel back toward him. Blood sprayed from his mouth as he bellowed, and teeth fell to the floor. Marsh ducked under the long barrel and came up with a hard punch to the jaw and another to the side of the head. Gomez staggered, eyes betraying that he still couldn't believe this odd duck had gotten the better of him.

Marsh wrenched the knife from a sheath around the Mexican's side as they grappled. Gomez flung himself away, knowing what would happen next. He collided with the rock wall, smashing shoulder and skull with a heavy groan. Marsh threw a punch which glanced off the Mexican and then hit rock. Blood seeped from his own knuckles. The gun came up again, but Marsh levered himself so that it rose between his legs, the business end now rendered useless.

Gomez head-butted him, their blood mingling and spraying the walls together. Marsh staggered but turned away from the next strike, and then remembered the knife still held in his left hand.

A powerful shove and the knife scraped Gomez's ribs, but the Mexican had dropped his gun and planted both hands on Marsh's knife arm, thus arresting the force and stopping the plunge of the blade. Pain twisted his features but the man had manage to halt certain death.

Marsh immediately concentrated on his free hand, using it to punch again and again, seeking out vulnerable areas. Together, the men struggled hard, inching up and down the tunnel, striking wooden beams and shuffling through mounds of dirt. Runnels of sweat hit the sand; heavy grunts like rutting pigs filled the man-made space. No quarter was given, but no ground was gained. Gomez took every punch like the hardened street fighter he was, and it was Marsh who started to weaken first.

"Look . . . forward to . . . cut . . . cutting you . . ." Gomez panted, eyes feral, lips bloody and flared back.

Marsh refused to die in this lonely, hellish place. He yanked the knife back, twisting it out of Gomez's body and then stepped back, giving the two men a few feet of separation. The gun lay on the floor, discarded.

Gomez came at him like a devil, screaming, rumbling. Marsh brushed the attack off as he had been taught to do, turning a shoulder and allowing Gomez's own momentum to slam him head first into the other wall. Then Marsh kicked him in the spine. He wouldn't use the knife again until the end was a foregone conclusion. He had also been taught that the most obvious weapon wasn't always the best one to use.

Gomez peeled his body off the wall, head hanging, and turned around. Marsh stared into the blood-red face of a demon. It fascinated him for a moment, the contrast of the crimson face and the white-fleshed neck, the black holes where yellowed teeth had once nestled, the pale ears sticking almost comically out to either side. Gomez swung a punch. Marsh took it on the side of the head.

Now Gomez was wide open.

Marsh stepped forward, head spinning, but retaining enough cognizance to thrust truly with the knife, sending its blade up into the other man's heart. Gomez jerked, breath whistling out of a shattered mouth, and then locked eyes with Marsh.

"I paid you with fair intentions," Marsh breathed. "You should have just taken the money."

These people, he knew, were traitorous by nature and no doubt by nurture too. Betrayal would be their second or third thought of the day, after "why is there blood on my hands?" and "who the hell did I end up killing last night?" Possibly a thought to the after-effects of a cocaine-blast in there as well. But Gomez . . . he should just have taken the money.

Marsh watched the man slither to the ground, then took stock. He was bruised, aching, but relatively unhurt. His head pounded. Luckily, he had thought to pack paracetamol in one of the backpack's small pouches that nestled alongside the nuke. So handy that. He had a pack of baby wipes in there too.

Marsh wiped and swallowed the tablets dry. He'd forgotten to pack water. *There's always something though, isn't there?*

Without a backward glance at the dead body he

lowered his head and began the long walk through the underground tunnel and into Texas.

The hours wore on. Julian Marsh trudged underneath America, a nuclear weapon strapped to his back. The device might be smaller than he'd expected—although it still bulged the backpack—but the internal gubbins were no less heavy. The thing dragged at him like an unwanted friend or brother, pulling him back. It made every step a strain.

Darkness surrounded and almost overwhelmed him, disrupted only by the occasional hanging light. Many were broken, too many. It was dank down here, the scuttle of unseen animals always painting nightmare images in his brain that played in wicked harmony to the random itches running across his shoulders and down his spine. Air was in limited supply, and what there was, was of poor quality.

He began to feel weary beyond measure, to hallucinate. Once, Tyler Webb chased him and then an evil troll. He fell twice, scraping knees and elbows, but dragged himself back to his feet. The troll transmogrified into evil Mexicans and then a walking taco, bursting with red and green peppers and guacamole.

As the miles wore on he began to feel that he might not make it, that everything would turn out better if he just lay down for a while. Take a little nap. The only thing stopping him was his more colorful side—the part that had once stubbornly survived childhood when everyone else wanted him to fade away.

Eventually brighter lights appeared ahead and he breached the other end of the tunnel, and then spent many minutes gauging what kind of a reception he might receive. In truth, he expected no reception committee—he'd never been expected to reach the land of the free.

By design, he'd arranged completely separate transport at this end. Marsh was careful, and no fool. A helicopter should be stationed a few miles off, awaiting his call. Marsh removed one of three burner cells secreted around his body and in the backpack, and made the call.

No words were passed when they met, no comments on the blood and dirt that encrusted Marsh's face and hair. The pilot lifted the bird into the air and swooped off in the direction of Corpus Christi—the next and penultimate stop in Marsh's grand adventure. One thing was for sure, he'd have a boatload of stories to tell . . .

And nobody to tell them to. One thing you didn't regale the party guests with was how you'd managed to smuggle a suitcase nuke from Brazil to the east coast of America.

Corpus Christi offered a little respite, a long shower and a quick nap. Next would be a twenty-four-hour drive to New York, and then . . .

Armageddon. Or at least the edge of it.

Marsh smiled as he rested face-down on the bed, head buried in a pillow. He could barely breathe but quite liked the feeling. The trick would be to convince the authorities that he was serious and that the bomb was authentic. Not hard—one look at the canisters and fissionable material would make them sit up and beg. Once that was done . . . Marsh imagined the dollars rolling in like some kind of Las Vegas slot machine throwing out money at a rate of knots. But all for a good cause. Webb's cause.

Maybe not. Marsh had his own plans to execute whilst the odd Pythian leader was off chasing rainbows.

He slithered off the bed, landing on his knees before rising. He applied a little lipstick. He rearranged the room's trappings so that they made sense. He exited and took an elevator to the basement where a rental awaited.

Chrysler 300. The size and color of a bleached whale.

Next stop . . . a city that never slept.

Marsh piloted the car effortlessly as the world-renowned skyline hove into view. It seemed ridiculously easy to take this car into New York, but then who knew any different? Well, somebody might. It had been over three days since he left Ramses' bazaar. What if news had leaked out? Marsh didn't change a thing. He was just one more traveler meandering his way through life. If the game was up he would find out very soon. Otherwise . . . Webb had promised that Ramses would provide men willing to help at this end. Marsh was counting on them.

Marsh drove blind, not knowing nor particularly caring what would happen next. He was cautious enough to stop before entering the great city, finding a night's refuge on the other side of the river as the sun began to set, adding to the unsystematic route of his journey. An L-shaped motel sufficed, though the bed linen was scratchy and undeniably unclean, and the window frames and floors edgings were inches thick with black grime. Still, it was unremarkable, unplanned and pretty much undetectable.

Which was why, around midnight, he sat up straight, heart pounding, as someone knocked at the door of his room. The door faced the parking lot, so in truth it could be anyone, from a lost drunken guest to a prankster. But it might also be the cops.

Or Seal Team Six.

Marsh arranged knives, spoons and glasses, and then brushed the curtain aside to peer outside. What he saw rendered him momentarily speechless.

What the . . . ?

The knock sounded again, light and breezy. Marsh didn't hesitate, but opened the door and allowed the person to step inside.

"You have surprised me," he said. "And that doesn't happen too often these days."

"I'm good that way," the visitor said. "One of my many attributes."

Marsh wondered about the others, but didn't have to look too far to spot at least a dozen. "We have only met once before."

"Yes. And I immediately sensed a kinship."

Marsh straightened his frame, now wishing he'd taken that fourth shower. "I thought all the Pythians were dead or captured. Apart from Webb and I."

"As you can see," the visitor spread her hands, "you were wrong."

"I'm pleased." Marsh offered a smile. "Very pleased.

"Oh," his visitor also smiled, "you're about to be."

Marsh tried to ward off the feeling that all his birthdays had come at once. This woman was odd, maybe as odd as himself. Her hair was brown and cut spiky; her eyes green and blue just like his own. How spooky was that? Her outfit consisted of a green woolen pullover, bright red jeans and dark blue Doc Martins. In one hand she held a glass of milk, in the other a glass of wine.

Where had she gotten . . . ?

But it didn't really matter. He liked that she was unique, that she somehow understood him. He liked that she'd turned up out of nowhere. He loved that she was entirely different. The forces of darkness were pushing them together. Blood red wine and bleach white milk were about to mix.

Marsh relieved her of the glasses. "You want to be on top, or on the bottom?"

"Oh, I don't mind. Let's see how the mood takes us."

So Marsh positioned the nuke at the head of the bed where they could both see it, seeing an additional spark flash comet-like through Zoe Sheers' eyes. This woman was powerful, deadly, and perfectly bizarre. Probably mad. Something that suited him no end.

As she stripped her clothes off, his dual mind wandered away to peruse what was to come. The thought of all the excitement promised for tomorrow and the next day as they brought America to its knees and played happy with the nuke made him perfectly ready for Zoe as she tugged his trousers down and climbed on board.

"No foreplay?" he asked.

"Well, when you placed that backpack just so," she said, watching the nuke as if it might be watching her. "I realized I didn't need it."

Marsh grinned with happy surprise. "Me too."

"You see, lover?" Zoe sank down onto him. "We were made for each other."

Marsh then realized he could see her slow-moving, extremely pale ass in the reflection of the mirror that hung on the wall just above the old dresser, and past that the backpack itself nestled among the bed's pillows. He stared into her well-tanned face.

"Damn," he blurted out. "This ain't gonna take long."

CHAPTER THREE

Matt Drake readied himself for the team's wildest ride yet. A nasty nauseating feeling thrashed in the pit of his stomach, and it had nothing to do with the bumpy flight, simply the product of tension, anxiety and disgust at the people who might try to perpetrate such horrendous crimes. He felt for the people of the world who went about their everyday business uninformed but contented. They were the people he fought for.

The choppers were chock-full of soldiers who cared and put themselves in harm's way for the people who made the world a good place to be. The entire SPEAR team was present, with the exception of Karin Blake and the addition of Beauregard Alain and Bridget McKenzie—aka Kenzie, the katana-wielding, artifact-smuggling, ex-Mossad agent. The team had departed Ramses' devastated last bazaar in such a hurry that they had been forced to bring everyone along with them. Not a minute could be wasted, and the whole team was prepped and informed and ready to hit New York's streets running.

From actual jungle to concrete jungle, Drake thought. *We never close.*

All around him sat the dependable crossed lines and turbulent waves of his life. Alicia and Beau, Mai and Kenzie, and Torsten Dahl. The second chopper housed Smyth and Lauren, Hayden, Kinimaka and

Yorgi. The team was speeding into New York's airspace, already cleared by President Coburn on down, and banking hard as they zipped through gaps between skyscrapers and zoomed low towards a square-shaped roof. Turbulence battered them. The radio squawked as information streamed in. Drake could only imagine the bustle on the streets below, the hurrying agents and frantic SWAT teams, the hellish thought of the sprint toward saving New York and the eastern seaboard.

He breathed deeply, sensing the next few hours would go ballistic.

Dahl caught his eye. "After this, I'm taking a vacation."

Drake admired the Swede's confidence. "After this, we're all gonna need one."

"Well, you ain't coming with me, Yorkie."

"Not a problem. I'm pretty sure Johanna will be in charge anyway."

"What the hell's that supposed to mean?"

The chopper fell fast, sending their stomachs toward the stratosphere.

Alicia sniggered. "Only that we know who runs the Dahl household, Torsty. We know."

The Swede made a face, but didn't comment further. Drake shared a grin with Alicia and then noticed Mai watching the both of them. *Shit, as if we didn't have enough to worry about.*

Alicia waved at Mai. "You sure you can handle this kinda action, Sprite, after cutting yourself shaving so recently?"

Mai's expression didn't change, but she did send a hesitant hand toward the new scar across her face. "Recent events have made me so much more careful about those people I trust. And to watch for those who betray."

Drake cringed inside.

Nothing has happened. She left me, ended it! Nothing was promised . . .

Emotions and thoughts churned together to make an acidic bile that mixed with a thousand other feelings. Dahl, he noticed, inched away from Kenzie, and Beau barely broke eye contact with Alicia. Christ, he hoped the passions were running a little lower inside the second chopper.

More wild winds battered them as the chopper's skids tapped against the building's roof. The bird settled and then the doors were flung open, occupants jumping down and sprinting to an open door. Men with guns guarded the entrance and several more were stationed inside. Drake ducked in first, feet flying and feeling a little unprepared without weapons, but knowing full well they would be tooling up soon. The team hustled down the narrow staircase one at a time until they emerged in a wide corridor, blacked out and lined by even more guards. Here, they paused for a moment before receiving instructions to continue.

All clear.

Drake jogged, aware they had lost vital days getting the information out of the bazaar and then being debriefed by suspicious agents, especially those from the CIA. In the end, it had been Coburn himself who intervened, commanding that the SPEAR team be sent immediately to the hottest spot on the planet.

New York City.

Now, down another flight of stairs and they came to a balcony area where they could look out over an inner set of rooms—the station house of a local police precinct on 3rd and 51st, he had been told. Unknown to the public the precinct doubled as a Homeland Security office—in fact it was one of two that had been called the city's "hub", the nucleus of all the agencies' activities. Now Drake watched the local police going about their everyday actions, the station bustling, loud and packed, before a black-suited man approached from the far end.

"Let's move," he said. "No time to waste here."

Drake couldn't agree more. He pushed Alicia along, much to the blonde's distaste, receiving a dour look for his troubles. The others crowded in, Hayden trying to approach the new guy but running out of time as he vanished through a far door. As they filed through they came into a round room with white tiled floor and walls, and chairs placed in rows facing a small dais. The man ushered them in as fast as he could.

"Thanks for coming," he said emotionlessly. "Just so you know the men you captured—the self-named Ramses, and Robert Price—have been taken to the cells below us, there to await the outcome of our . . . manhunt. We figured they might hold valuable information and should be close by."

"Especially if we fail," Alicia said grimly.

"Indeed. And these prison cells, underground, with added security inside the Homeland division, will keep Ramses' presence undetected, as I'm sure you can appreciate."

Drake remembered that Ramses' local units, after they had stolen or violently taken the nuke from Marsh's hands, were under orders to await Ramses' go ahead for detonation. They didn't know he had been captured, or that he'd almost died. The New York cells of Ramses' organization knew nothing at all.

It was at least one thing the SPEAR team had in their favor.

"He will become useful," Hayden said. "I'm pretty sure."

"Yeah," Smyth added. "So lay off the cattle prod for now."

The Homeland agent winced. "My name is Moore. I am the lead field agent here. All intelligence will pass through me. We're setting up a new task force to assimilate and assign actions. We have the hub, and now we're arranging the offshoots. Every agent and cop—available or not—is working this threat and we are fully aware of the consequences of failure. This cannot . . ." he faltered a little, showing stress which would normally be unheard of. "This cannot be allowed to happen here."

"Who is in charge on the ground?" Hayden asked. "Who makes the decisions here, where it really counts?"

Moore hesitated and scratched his chin. "Well, we do. Homeland. In conjunction with the Counter

Terrorism Unit and the Threat Squad."

"And by we do you mean you and I? Or do you mean just Homeland?"

"I think that may change as the situation demands," Moore allowed.

Hayden looked satisfied. "Make sure your cellphone battery's charged."

Moore looked the group over, as if sensing their urgency and liking it. "We have a short window as you know. It won't take long for these bastards to figure out Ramses ain't about to lay down that order. So, first things first. How do we locate a terrorist cell?"

Drake checked his watch. "And Marsh. Shouldn't Marsh be the priority since he's with the bomb?"

"Intelligence says Marsh will merge with the local cells. We don't know how many that will be. So we concentrate on both, of course."

Drake recalled Beau's report of the conversation between Marsh and Webb. It occurred to him then that the slippery Frenchman, whom they first met whilst being forced to participate in the Last Man Standing tourney and pretty much battled against ever since, had shone for the light of good when it mattered. Shone like a star. He really should give the guy an extra break.

Somewhere along the tibia . . .

Moore spoke again. "There are several ways to locate a deep cell, or even a sleeper cell. We narrow the suspect pool. We investigate links to other known cells that are already under surveillance. Check fiery places of worship where well-known Jihadists spew their poison. We look at newly ritualized people—those who suddenly develop interests in religion, withdraw from society or speak out about a woman's dress. The NSA listens to metadata collected from millions of cellphones, and evaluates. But far more effective are the men and women who risk it every day of the week—those we have infiltrated into the population from which fresh Jihadists are regularly recruited."

"Undercover." Smyth nodded. "That's good."

"It is. Our information thus far is thinner than Barbie Iggy Pop. We're trying to confirm the amount of people in each cell. Size of cells. Areas. Capabilities and readiness. We're combing all the recent phone logs. Do you think Ramses will talk?"

Hayden was itching to get started. "We're gonna give it a friggin' good try."

"The threat is imminent," Kinimaka said. "Let's assign teams and get the hell out there."

"Yes, yes, that's good," Moore explained. "But where will you go? New York is a very large city. Nothing can be gained by running off without a place to go. We don't even know if the bomb is real. Many people can make a bomb . . . look right."

Alicia shifted in her seat. "I can vouch for that."

"Vehicles are at the ready," Moore said. "SWAT vehicles. Choppers. Unmarked, fast cars. Believe it or not we do have plans for this scenario, ways to clear the streets. Officials and their families are already being evacuated. All we require now is a starting point."

Hayden turned to her team. "So let's quickly assign groups and get started on Ramses. Like the man said—our window is small and it's already closing."

CHAPTER FOUR

Julian Marsh left the motel feeling refreshed, even exhilarated but also a little sad. He'd dressed well; blue jeans with one leg a tad darker than the other, several layers of shirts and a hat tugged down over one side of his head. The look was good, and he thought he'd outdone Zoe. The woman emerged from the little bathroom looking a bit disheveled, hair only partly brushed and lipstick half-applied. It was only after a few minutes of appraisal that Marsh realized she was deliberately trying to emulate him.

Or pay tribute to him?

Probably the latter, but it did set Marsh on edge. The last thing he wanted was a female version of himself cramping his unique style. Almost as an afterthought he plucked the backpack from the bed, stroking the material and feeling the contours of the living beast inside.

Mine.

The morning felt good, crisp, bright and happy. Marsh waited as a five-seater car pulled up and two men jumped out of the front. Both were swarthy and bore full beards. Marsh spoke the final password for the final journey and allowed them to open the back door. Zoe appeared as he climbed in.

"Wait." One of the men produced a pistol as the woman approached. "There should be only one."

Marsh tended to agree, but a different side of him wanted to get to know the woman even better. "She is a late addition. She's okay."

Still the gun hand hesitated.

"Look, I have been out of contact for three days, maybe four." Marsh couldn't clearly recall. "Plans change. I gave you the password, now heed my words. She's okay. An asset, even."

"Very well." Neither man looked convinced.

The car took off fast, spinning a plume of dirt from the rear tires, and turned toward the city. Marsh settled back as the skyscrapers loomed even larger and the traffic thickened. Shiny, reflective surfaces surrounded the car, blinding in some places as they redirected the artificial lights. Crowds thronged the sidewalks and buildings flashed with information. Cop cars cruised the streets. Marsh saw no sign of heightened police attention, but then couldn't see above the roof of the car. He mentioned it to the driver.

"Everything seems normal," the man came back. "But speed is still essential. Everything will fall apart if we move too slowly."

"Ramses?" Marsh asked.

"We await his word."

Marsh frowned, sensing some condescension in the reply. This plan was entirely his and Ramses' minions should be dancing to his tune. As soon as they arrived at the place Marsh had chosen and prepped months before they could begin.

"Stay under the radar," he said by way of asserting

control. "And under the speed limit, eh? We don't want to get stopped."

"We are in New York," the driver said, and then both men laughed as he gunned it from a red light. Marsh chose to ignore them.

"But," the driver then added. "Your backpack? It's . . . contents have to be verified."

"I know that," Marsh hissed. "Don't you think I know that?"

What type of ape had Webb saddled him with?

Perhaps sensing the rising tensions, Zoe sidled over toward him. Only the nuke sat between them. Her hand wriggled slowly over the backpack, a fingertip at a time, and down toward his lap, making him start and then stare.

"Is that really appropriate?"

"I don't know, Julian. Is it?"

Marsh wasn't entirely sure, but the sensations were pleasant enough so he let it go. It occurred to him briefly that Sheers was a bit of a looker, powerful as a Shadow Pope, and no doubt able to call upon any male specimen she required.

Why me?

The nuke probably helped, he knew. Every girl fancied a man with a nuke. Something to do with power . . . oh, well, maybe she liked the idea that he was that little bit more formidable than her. His quirkiness? Sure, why the hell not? His train of thought derailed as they pulled up at the curb, the driver briefly pointing out the building that Marsh had chosen on a previous visit. Outside, the day was still warm and entirely unexpected. Marsh imagined fat government asses planted firmly in their plush leather seats about to get the spanking of their lives.

Soon now. So soon I can barely contain myself.

He took Zoe by the hand and pretty much skipped across the sidewalk, letting the backpack dangle from a crooked elbow. Past the doorman and with instructions left, the four-strong group took an elevator to the fourth floor and then checked the spacious, two-bedroom apartment. All was well. Marsh threw open the balcony doors and took another sniff of the city air.

Might as well whilst I still can.

The irony made him laugh at himself. It would never happen. All the Americans had to do was believe, pay up, and then he could dispose of the nuke in the Hudson as planned. Then, a new plan. A new life. And a fascinating future.

A voice spoke at his shoulder. "We have a man on the way who is able to verify the contents of your backpack. He should arrive within the hour."

Marsh nodded without turning. "As expected. Very good. But there are still a few considerations. I need a boffin to help with the money transfer once the White House has paid. I need help setting the chase in motion, to help divert attentions. And we need to activate all the cells and arm that bomb."

The man behind him shifted. "All in the planning," he said. "We are prepared. These things will come together very soon."

Marsh turned and walked back into the hotel room.

Zoe sat sipping champagne, her slim legs raised and resting along a chaise longue. "So we're just waiting now?" he asked the guy.

"Not long."

Marsh smiled at Zoe and held out a hand. "We'll be in the bedroom."

The couple snagged a strap each of the backpack and carried it with them into the biggest bedroom. Within a minute they were both naked and twisting together atop the sheets. Marsh tried to prove he possessed the required reserves of stamina this time, but Zoe was just a little too wily. Her wide flawless face did all sorts of things to his libido. In the end it was good that Marsh finished quickly because there soon came a knock at the bedroom door.

"The man is here."

Already? Marsh dressed quickly alongside Zoe and then the two of them wandered back out into the suite, still flushed and slightly sweating. Marsh shook hands with the newcomer, noting his lank hair, pale complexion and rumpled clothes.

"Don't get out much?"

"They keep me locked away."

"Oh, well, whatever. Have you come to check my bomb?"

"Yes, sir, I have."

Marsh placed the backpack on the low glass table that occupied the center of the large room. Zoe walked by, catching his attention as he briefly remembered her naked form from only minutes ago. He dragged his eyes away, addressing the newcomer.

"What's your name, lad?"

"Adam, sir."

"Well, Adam, you know what this is and what it can do. Do you feel nervous?"

"No, not at the moment."

"Tense?"

"I don't think so."

"Twitchy? Stressed? Maybe overwrought?"

Adam shook his head, eyeing the backpack.

"If you are I'm sure Zoe here can help you out." He said it half-jokingly.

The Pythian turned with a sly smile. "Be happy to."

Marsh blinked, as did Adam, but before the youth changed his mind their bearded driver spoke up. "Hurry this," he said. "We must be ready for . . ." he tailed off.

Marsh shrugged. "All right, no need to start stamping your feet. Let's get down and dirty." He turned to Adam. "With the bomb, I mean."

The young man turned a bewildered gaze firmly upon the backpack and then rotated it, so the buckles faced him. Slowly, he undid them and eased the top open. Inside lay the real device, surrounded by a sturdier and altogether superior backpack.

"Okay," Adam said. "So we all know about MASINT, the Measurement and Signature Intelligence protocol that scans data received from radiation and other physical phenomena signatures associated with nukes. This device, and at least one other like it that I know of, have been post-designed to slip under that field. Now, there are a lot of systems detecting and monitoring the world for nuclear devices but not all of them are cutting edge, and not all of them are fully manned." He shrugged. "Look at the recent debacles in civilized countries. Can anyone really stop a determined man or tight cell acting alone? Of course not. It only takes a single malfunction or an inside job." He smiled. "An unhappy employee or even a dead-tired one. Mostly it takes money or leverage. These are the best currencies of international terrorism."

Marsh listened to the young man talk, wondering if one or two deeper precautions had been taken when he explained his route to Ramses and Webb. It would have been in all their best interests. He would never know and, frankly, didn't really care. He was right here now, and about to open the doorway to Hell.

"Essentially, this is what we call a 'dirty bomb'," Adam said. "The term has been around forever but still applies. I have a scintillometer to detect alpha particles, a contaminant detector, and a few other goodies. But mostly," Adam took a screwdriver out of his pocket, "I have this."

Quickly he removed the sturdy package and unstickered the Velcro straps that gave access to a small display and mini-keyboard. The panel was held down by four screws which Adam quickly removed. As the metal panel came free it unraveled a series of wires behind it, wires that ran into the heart of the newly revealed device.

Marsh held his breath.

Adam smiled for the first time. "Don't worry. This

thing has more than one failsafe and ain't even armed yet. Nobody here will set it off."

Marsh felt a little deflated.

Adam peered at the mechanism and the parts inside it, taking it all in. After a moment he checked a laptop screen at his side. "Leaking," he admitted. "But not so bad."

Marsh shifted uneasily. "How bad?"

"I'd advise you never to have kids," Adam said without emotion. "If you still can. And enjoy the next few years of your life."

Marsh stared at Zoe as she shrugged. He'd never expected to outlive his egotistical father nor his supercilious brothers anyway.

"I can shield it better now," Adam said, taking a package from a suitcase he'd brought along with him. "As I would any device of this sort."

Marsh watched for a moment and then realized they were almost done. He met the dead eyes of their driver. "These cells Ramses spoke of. Are they ready? The chase will soon start and I want no delays."

A dry smile flickered back. "And neither do we. All five cells are now active, including the two sleepers that the Americans cannot possibly know of." The man checked his watch. "It is now 6.45 a.m. All will be ready for seven."

"Fantastic." Marsh felt his libido rising again and thought he might as well take advantage of that fact whilst he still could. Knowing Zoe as he recently did, they'd finish quickly anyway. "And the money transfer protocols?"

"Adam will concentrate on finishing a program that will bounce our location around the world on an endless cycle. They will never track the transaction."

Marsh didn't notice Adam's expression of surprise.

He was too concentrated on Zoe, and she on him. He took five more minutes to watch Adam arm the bomb and listen to the instructions on how to disarm the damn thing, and then made sure the man took the relevant photographs of the working device. The photographs were crucial in persuading the White House of the authenticity of the device and in engineering the chase that would divert attentions and divide the forces arrayed against him. Happy at last he addressed Adam.

"The yellow one. That's the disarm wire?"

"Umm, yes sir, it is."

Marsh turned a genuine smile upon the driver. "So we're ready?"

"We are ready."

"Then move out."

Marsh held out a hand and led Zoe into the bedroom, tugging at her jeans and panties as they went, and trying to stifle a giggle. A flood of passion and excitement almost overwhelmed him as he realized all his dreams of power and importance were about to be realized. If only his family could see him now.

CHAPTER FIVE

As Drake stood upright the full weight of what was transpiring bore down upon him. Urgency coursed through his veins, frayed his nerve-endings, and one look at his team-mates told him they felt the same— even Kenzie. He'd really thought the ex-Mossad agent would have made her move by now but then, in truth, because of the bond between soldiers, he didn't even have to ask her why she hadn't. The same innocents she fought for were at stake here, the same civilians. Anyone with even half a heart would not let this stand, and Drake suspected there might be a lot more to Kenzie than half a heart, however deeply buried it may be.

Seven-forty-five, the wall clock read and the whole team were on the move. The police station was filled with an uneasy chaotic calm, cops in charge but clearly on edge. News reports flashed across TV screens, but none that were relevant to them. Moore paced and paced, waiting for news from undercover agents or surveillance teams or roving cars. Hayden squared off with the rest of the team.

"Mano and I will handle Ramses. We need two more groups, one to evaluate the nuke information as it happens, and one to chase down these cells. Keep everything quiet, but take no prisoners. Today, my friends, is not a day for fucking around. Get what you need and get it fast and hard. A lie could cost us dearly."

Moore picked up on what she was saying and looked over. "Today," he said, "there will be no quarter."

Dahl nodded grimly as he cracked knuckles like he might a man's skull. Drake tried to relax. Even Alicia marched around like a caged panther.

Then, at 8 a.m., the craziness began.

Calls started to come in, dedicated phones ringing again and again, their clamor filling the small room. Moore fielded them with efficiency, one after another, and two assistants ran in to help. Even Kinimaka took a call, though the table he perched on didn't sound particularly happy.

Moore collated the information at the speed of light. "We're on," he said. "All teams are go. Undercovers have reported back the most recent talk of secret meetings and chatter. Movements around known mosques have ramped up. Even if we didn't know what was going on we'd be worried. New faces have been seen in the usual haunts, all determined and moving fast, purposefully. Of the cells we know about two have disappeared off the radar." Moore shook his head. "As if we weren't already up against it. But we have leads. One team should head to the docks—one of the known cells operates from there."

"That's us," Dahl grated. "Mount up, motherfuckers."

"Speak for yourself." Kenzie sidled alongside. "Oh, and I'm with you."

"Ahh, do you have to?"

"Stop playing hard to get."

Drake studied the teams, which had paired off quite interestingly. Dahl and Kenzie had Lauren, Smyth and Yorgi as comrades. He had ended up with Alicia, Mai and Beau. It was a recipe for something; that was for sure.

"Good luck, mate," Drake said.

Dahl turned to say something just as Moore held a hand up. "Wait!" He covered the receiver for a second. "This was just patched through to our hotline."

All heads swiveled. Moore had fielded another call and was now sending a hand out, scrabbling for the speaker button.

"You're on," Moore said.

A disembodied crackle filled the room, the words spilling as fast as Drake's legs wanted to run in pursuit. "This is Julian Marsh, and I know that you know almost everything. Yes, I do. The question is—how would you like to play it?"

Hayden took point as Moore waved for a trace. "Stop dicking about, Marsh. Where is it?"

"Well, that's the explosive question, isn't it? I'll tell you this, my dear, it's here. In New York City."

Drake didn't dare breathe as their worst fears were undeniably confirmed.

"So the other question is—what do I want next?" Marsh allowed a long pause.

"Get to it, asshole," Smyth snarled.

Alicia frowned. "Let's not antagonize the prick."

Marsh laughed. "Let's not, indeed. So the nuke is

armed, the codes all nicely entered. Clock is ticking, as they say. Now all that needs to be done is verify that it is real and provide you with a bank account number. Am I right?"

"Yes," Hayden said simply.

"You want proof? You're gonna have to work for it."

Drake leaned forward. "What do you mean?"

"I mean the chase is on."

"Will you be getting to the point anytime soon?" Hayden asked.

"Ah, we'll get to it. First, you little worker ants have a job to do. I'd get scuttling if I were you. You see . . . you see how I made that rhyme? I was going to make everything rhyme, you know, but in the end . . . well, I realized that I didn't give that much of a fuck."

Drake shook his head in despair. "Bloody 'ell, mate. Speak proper English."

"The first clue is already in play. A form of verification. You have twenty minutes to get to the Hotel Edison, Room 201. Then there will be four more clues, some of verification and some of demands. Do you get me now?"

Mai came back first. "Insanity."

"Well, I am a man of two minds. One of need, one of vice. Perhaps at their intersection sparks of madness fly."

"Twenty minutes?" Drake checked his watch. "Can we even make it?"

"For every minute you are late I have ordered one of Ramses' cells to kill two civilians."

Again the jaw-dropping shock, the terror, the

mounting suspense. Drake clenched his fists as the adrenaline rose.

"Twenty minutes," Marsh reiterated. "From . . . now."

Drake sprinted out the door.

Hayden raced down the stairs and towards the building's basement, Kinimaka at her back. Fury rode her and beat at her as if with a devil's wings. Anger forced her legs to go faster and almost caused her to trip. Her Hawaiian partner grunted, slipped and picked himself up almost without stopping. She thought about her friends in dire peril, rushing off to different areas of the city with no idea of what to expect, laying themselves on the line without question. She thought about all the civilians out there and what the White House might now be thinking. It was all well and good to have protocols and plans and workable formulas, but when the real, working world became the object of extreme threat—all bets were off. At the bottom of the stairs she hit a corridor and sprinted. Doors flashed by to either side, most unlit. At the far end a row of bars were quickly slid aside for her.

Hayden held her hand out. "Gun."

The guard flinched, but then acquiesced, orders from above having already reached his ears.

Hayden took the weapon, checked the thing was loaded and the safety was off, and burst into the small room.

"Ramses!" she shouted. "What the hell have you done?"

CHAPTER SIX

Drake dashed out of the building, Alicia, Mai and Beau at his side. Sweat already soaked the four of them. Determination sprang from every pore. Beau fished a state-of-the-art GPS out of a pocket and pinpointed the Edison.

"Times Square area," he said, studying the route. "Across third and over Lexington Avenue. Make for the Waldorf Astoria."

Drake raced into plodding traffic. There was nothing like trying to save the life of a New York cabbie as he tried desperately to break your legs at the knees, inching forward as best he could. Drake jumped at the last second, sliding over the front of the closest yellow cab and landing in full flow. Horns blared. Each member of the team had managed to commandeer a handgun on the way out and brandished them now whilst wishing they had more. But time was already wasting away. Drake checked his watch as he hit the sidewalk.

Seventeen minutes.

They crossed Lexington and then ran alongside the Waldorf, barely stopping as the cars along Park Avenue crawled along. Drake fought his way through a crowd at the traffic signal, finally confronted by an angry, red face.

"Look, buddy, I'm crossing here first if it kills me.

Bosses' bagels gonna get cold and that's a damn no-no."

Drake skirted the angry individual as Alicia and Mai burst past on the outside. The signals changed and the road was clear. Now with guns concealed they headed hard for the next main street—Madison Avenue. Again the crowds thronged the sidewalk. Beau skipped out onto 49th, hopping between cars and gaining a lead. Luckily, the traffic was now moving slowly and afforded them clear spaces in between rear bumpers and front fenders. The women followed Beau and then Drake fell into line.

Drivers shouted abuse at them.

Twelve minutes left.

If they were late, where would the terrorist cells strike? Drake imagined it would be in proximity to the Edison. Marsh would want the team to know his orders had been carried out to the letter. A car door opened ahead—just because the driver could—and Beau leaped over the top just in time. Alicia took hold of the edge of the frame and slammed it back into the man's face.

Now they cut to the left, approaching 5th Avenue and even more crowds. Beau slipped through the worst of it like a pickpocket at a pop concert, followed by Alicia and Mai. Drake just shouted at everyone, his Yorkshireman's patience finally running out. Both men and women blocked his path—men and women who didn't give a rat's shit whether he might be rushing to save his own life, one of his children's, or even theirs. Drake muscled his way through, leaving one man sprawling. A woman with a baby glared at him hard enough to make him feel guilty, until he remembered what he was running for.

You'll thank me later.

But, of course, she would never know. Whatever happened.

Now Beau shot left, running down the Avenue of the Americas towards 47th Street. A Magnolia Bakery passed by on the right, making Drake think of Mano, and then what the Hawaiian might have gleaned from Ramses by now. Two minutes later and they were blasting up 47th, Times Square suddenly visible to their left. The customary Starbucks sat to their right, bustling and queuing out the door. Drake scanned faces as he dashed by, but didn't expect to come face to face with any suspects.

Four minutes.

Time was spinning away faster and even more precious than the last moments of a dying old man. The hotel's gray façade and golden entrance appeared to the left, fronting the sidewalk, and Beau was the first to swing through the front doors. Drake skirted a luggage trolley and a dangerously reversing yellow cab to follow Mai inside. A wide foyer and patterned red carpet greeted them.

Beau and Alicia were already pressing the call buttons for separate elevators, hands close to concealed weapons, as a security guard watched them. Drake thought about producing the SPEAR team ID card, but it would only lead to more questions and the countdown was already inside the final three minutes.

A chime announced that Alicia's elevator had arrived and the team piled on. Drake stopped a young man from joining them, warding him off with an open palm. Thank God that worked, because the next gesture would have been a closed fist.

The four-strong team gathered themselves as the car rose, shaking off the run and drawing weapons. Once the door opened they piled out, searching for room 201. Instantly, a whirlwind of fists and legs was among them, shocking even Beau.

Somebody had been waiting.

Drake flinched as a fist connected above his eye socket but ignored the flash of pain. A foot tried to sweep his own but he sidestepped. The same figure moved away and beset Alicia, slamming her frame into the plastered wall. Mai stopped blows with raised hands and then Beau struck fast, a one-two that stopped all momentum and drove their attacker to his knees.

Drake leapt up and then punched downward with all his strength. Time was ebbing away. The figure, a chunky man wearing a thick jacket, shuddered under the Yorkshireman's blow, but somehow managed to deflect the worst of it. Drake fell to the side, unbalanced.

"A punching bag," Mai said. "He's a punching bag. Positioned to slow us down."

Beau drove in harder than before. "He is mine. You go."

Drake jumped over the kneeling figure, checking room numbers. Their destination sat only three rooms away and they had one minute left. They were down to the final seconds. Drake paused outside the room and kicked at the door. Nothing happened.

Mai pushed him aside. "Move."

One high kick and the wood splintered, a second and the frame collapsed. Drake coughed. "Must have weakened it for you."

Inside, they spread out, guns ready and searching quickly but the object they sought was terribly obvious. It lay in the middle of the bed—an A4 size glossy photograph. Alicia approached the bed, staring from side to side.

"The room is immaculate," Mai said. "No clues, I will bet."

Alicia paused at the side of the bed, looking down and breathing shallowly. She shook her head and groaned as Drake joined her.

"Oh God. Is that a—"

The ringing telephone interrupted him. Drake leapt around the bed to the nightstand and snatched the receiver from the cradle.

"Yes!"

"Ah, I see you made it. Couldn't have been easy."

"Marsh! You crazy bastard. You've left us a photograph of the bomb? A fucking photograph?"

"Yes. Your first clue. Why, did you think I'd let you have the real thing? So stupid. Send it to your leaders and your eggheads. They will verify the serial numbers and all that other rubbish. The canisters of Plutonium E. The fissionable material. Boring stuff, really. The next clue will be even more telling."

At that moment Beau entered the room. Drake was hoping he would be dragging Punchbag Man along with him but Beau drew an imaginary line across his carotid. "He killed himself," the Frenchman said in a bemused voice. "Suicide pill."

Shit.

"You see?" Marsh said. "We are very serious."

"Please, Marsh," Drake tried. "Just tell us what you want. We'll do it right bloody now."

"Oh, I'm sure you would. But we'll save that for later, eh? How about this? Get running for clue number two. This chase is getting better and more difficult. You have twenty minutes to reach the Marea restaurant. It's Italian, by the way and they make a mighty mean Nduju calzone, believe me. But no stopping for that, my friends, because this clue you will find placed under a toilet bowl. Enjoy."

"Marsh—"

"Twenty minutes."

The line went dead.

Drake cursed, turned, and ran like hell.

CHAPTER SEVEN

With no other option, Torsten Dahl and his team decided to dump the car and hoof it. He'd have liked nothing better than to hang on tight as Smyth threw a powerful SUV around half a dozen corners, tires squealing, objects shifting, but New York at this time was nothing but an angry snarl of yellow cabs, buses and hire cars. Gridlock was the word that entered Dahl's mind, but it happened every day, most of the day, and still the horns blared and men shouted out of lowered windows. They ran hard, following directions. Lauren and Yorgi had shrugged into flak jackets. Kenzie jogged alongside Dahl, face turned down into a pout.

"I'd be of much more use to you," she said to Dahl.

"No."

"Oh, come on, how can it hurt?"

"Not a chance."

"Oh, Torsty—"

"Kenzie, you are not getting your bloody katana back. And don't call me that. Having one crazy woman assigning me nicknames is bad enough."

"Oh, yeah? So did you and Alicia ever . . . you know?"

Smyth growled as they crossed another intersection, seeing pedestrians and bikes cramming the road at a green light, all taking their lives in their hands, but confident it wouldn't be them who got hurt today. Quickly, they raced down the next street, soldiers barely feeling the burn of the sprint as they whipped around two slow-moving Prius's, smashing wing mirrors. The GPS bleeped.

"Four minutes to the docks," Yorgi estimated. "We should slow down."

"I'll slow down in three," Smyth snapped. "Don't tell me my job."

Dahl handed Kenzie a Glock and a HK, not an easy task to perform covertly in New York. He winced as he did so. Against his better judgment they had practically been forced to accept the rogue agent's help. This was no ordinary day and all measures, even desperate ones, were required. And truth be told, he still felt they might share a kinship, something of parallel military souls, which increased his level of trust.

He believed they might be able to save Bridget McKenzie no matter how hard she resisted.

Now Smyth veered across two lanes of traffic, shoulder-swiping a stalled F150 but continuing without a glance back. With no time they could afford no courtesies, and the terrible cloud hanging over them meant they were being forced to go all in, all of the time.

Dahl cocked his weapons. "Warehouse is less than a minute away," he said. "And why the hell don't they sort all these potholes?"

Smyth sympathized with him. The roads were an unending, pockmarked, hazardous tract where cars inched around jagged holes and roadworks were thrown up at any moment, seemingly uncaring of the time of day or density of traffic. It really was dog eat dog out there, with no man looking to help any other.

Quickly, they took their bearings from the GPS and aimed for the tip of the arrow. Early morning crispness threw pins and needles at their exposed skin, reminding them all it was still early. Sunlight filtered through breaks in the clouds, bathing the docks and the nearby river in pale gold. Those men that Dahl could see went about their business as usual. He'd imagined the dock area to be dark and dingy but apart from the warehouses the area was clean, and not particularly crowded. Nor was it busy, as the major shipping areas were across the bay in New Jersey. Still, Dahl saw large, battered containers and a long wide vessel stationary on the waters and enormous blue-painted container cranes that could traverse the length of the quay on rail tracks and collect their containers with spreaders.

Warehouses sat to the left, along with a yard full of more brightly colored containers. Dahl pointed to a building one hundred and fifty feet away.

"That's our boy. Smyth, Kenzie, come forward. I want Lauren and Yorgi behind us."

He moved off, focused now, concentrating on getting one assault behind them before they moved on to the next . . . and then the next until this nightmare was over and he could return to his family. Newly painted doors were dotted along the side of the building, and Dahl raised his head at the first window.

"Empty office. Let's try the next."

Minutes passed as the group crept along the side of the building, guns drawn, trying window after window, door after door. Dahl noticed with frustration that they were beginning to attract attention from the local workers. He didn't want to spook their quarry.

"C'mon."

They hurried along, finally reaching the fifth window along and taking a quick look. Dahl saw a wide space cluttered by cardboard boxes and wooden crates, but close to the window he also saw a rectangular table. Around the table sat four men, heads down as if they were talking, planning and thinking. Dahl dropped down and crouched with his back to the wall.

"We good?" Smyth asked.

"Possible," Dahl said. "Could be nothing . . . but—"

"I trust you," Kenzie said with a modicum of sarcasm. "You lead, I'll follow," Then she shook her head. "You people are really that mad? Just burst in there and start the shooting first?"

A man was approaching, squinting at them. Dahl raised his HK and the man froze, hands shooting up into the air. The decision was made mostly because the guy stood in the direct eye line of anyone inside the warehouse. Less than a second passed before Dahl rose, spun, and smashed a shoulder against the outer door. Smyth and Kenzie were with him, reading his thoughts.

As Dahl entered the spacious warehouse, four men jumped up from the table. Guns rested by their sides, and they withdrew them now, firing indiscriminately at the incoming strangers. Bullets flew everywhere, shattering the window and smashing through the swinging door. Dahl dived headlong, rolling, coming up firing. The men from the table scrambled away as they shot back, shooting over shoulders and even between their legs as they ran. Nowhere was safe. Errant gunfire filled the cavernous space. Dahl scrabbled on both elbows until he reached the table and upended it, using it as a shield. One end shattered as a high-caliber round passed straight through.

"Shit."

"Are you trying to get me killed?" Kenzie muttered.

The big Swede changed tactics, picked up the huge table, and then launched it through the air. The tumbling edges caught one man around the ankles, sending him flying and his gun scudding away. As Dahl approached fast, Kenzie's voice made him slow down.

"Careful with these little fuckers. I've worked all over the Middle East and seen a thousand of 'em wearing vests."

Dahl hesitated. "I don't think you can just—"

The explosion rocked the warehouse walls. The Swede flew off his feet, airborne, and smashed into the already devastated window. White noise filled his head, the overwhelming buzz of tinnitus, and for a second he couldn't see. By the time his vision started to clear he was aware of Kenzie crouched before him, patting his cheeks.

"Wake up, man. It wasn't the entire body, just a grenade."

"Oh. Well that makes me feel better."

"This is our chance," she said. "The concussion knocked his idiot comrades down too."

Dahl struggled to his feet. Smyth was up, but Lauren and Yorgi sat on their knees, fingers pressed to their temples. Dahl saw the terrorists starting to recover. Urgency pricked at him like a prong poking a piece of tenderized meat. Raising his gun he came under fire again but managed to wound one of the rising terrorists, and watched the man twist and fall.

Smyth raced past. "Got him."

Dahl forged ahead. Kenzie squeezed off shots beside him. The two remaining terrorists turned a corner and Dahl realized they were headed outside. He slowed momentarily, then turned the same corner, firing carefully, but his bullets hit only empty air and concrete. The door was wide open.

A grenade bounced back inside.

The explosion was a matter of course now, the SPEAR team taking cover and waiting for the shrapnel to pass them by. Walls shuddered and cracked under an intense impact. Then they were up, squeezing out the door in cover formation and into the brightening day.

"One o clock," Smyth said.

Dahl stared in the direction indicated, saw two running figures and, beyond them, the Hudson leading to the Upper Bay. "Bollocks, they may have speedboats."

Kenzie dropped to one knee, sighting carefully. "Then we take—"

"No," Dahl pushed her weapon's barrel downward.

"Can't you see the civilians over there?"

"Zubi," she cursed in Hebrew, a language Dahl had no understanding of. Together, Smyth, Kenzie and the Swede started a pursuit. The terrorists were quick, almost at the dockside already. Kenzie compromised by firing her HK into the air, expecting the civilians to either scatter or take cover.

"You can thank me after we save the day," she barked.

Dahl saw an avenue of opportunity open up. Both terrorists were standing tall against a watery background, great targets, and Kenzie's opportunistic fire had cleared the way. He slowed and fitted the stock to his shoulder, taking careful aim. Smyth followed suit at his side.

The terrorists turned as if practicing telepathy, already shooting. Dahl kept his focus as lead whizzed between the SPEAR team. His second bullet took his target in the chest, his third in the forehead, dead-center. The man toppled backwards, already dead.

"Keep one alive," Lauren's voice came through his earpiece.

Smyth fired. The last terrorist had already jumped aside, the bullet tugging at his jacket as Smyth adjusted. A swift movement saw the terrorist hurl another grenade—this one along the dockside itself.

"No!" Dahl fired fruitlessly, his heart leaping up into his throat.

The small bomb exploded with a loud report, the blast wave echoing across the docks. Dahl leapt behind a container for a moment and then sprang back out—but his momentum faltered as he saw there was now more than the remaining terrorist to worry about.

One of the container cranes had been damaged by the blast at its base, and was listing dangerously above the riverside. The sounds of screeching, tearing metal heralded an inevitable collapse. Men stared up and started running away from the high framework.

The terrorist took out another grenade.

"Not this time, asswipe." Smyth was already poised on one knee, squinting along his sights. He squeezed the trigger, watching the last terrorist fall before he could pull the pin on the grenade.

But there was no stopping the crane. Leaning, slanting, and collapsing all along its frame, the heavy iron scaffold crashed down upon the dockside, destroying the skeleton and pulverizing the small hut it fell upon. Containers were damaged and moved backward several feet. Bars and spars of metal bounced down, rebounding off the ground like deadly matchsticks. A bright blue pole the size of a street light careened between Smyth and Dahl—something that could have broken them in half had it hit—and came to a halt only feet away from where Lauren and Yorgi stood with their backs to the warehouse.

"No go." Kenzie sighted on the terrorist, double-checking. "He's very dead."

Dahl gathered his wits and surveyed the docks. A quick check showed that mercifully nobody had been hurt by the container crane. He placed a finger to his throat mic.

"Cell down," he said. "But they're all dead."

Lauren came back. "All right, I'll pass it on."

Kenzie's hand fell across Dahl's shoulder. "You should have let me take the shot. I would have taken the bastard's knees out; then we would have made him talk, one way or another."

"Too risky." Dahl understood why she didn't get it. "And it's doubtful we could have made him talk in the short time we have."

Kenzie huffed. "You speak for Europe and America. I am Israeli."

Lauren came back over the comms. "We have to go. There's been a cell sighting. Not good."

Dahl, Smyth and Kenzie hijacked the nearest vehicle, figuring if it only took them five minutes further than walking, the time-saving could be more than crucial.

CHAPTER EIGHT

Drake struck the concrete of 47th Street, running flat out with only eighteen minutes left on the clock. Immediately they were presented with a problem.

"Seventh, Eighth or Broadway?" Mai shouted.

Beau waved the GPS at her. "Marea is close to Central Park."

"Yes, but which street leads us right past it?"

They hovered at the sidewalk whilst the seconds ticked away, knowing Marsh was readying not only the nuke, but also the teams who would take two civilian lives for every minute they were late to the next rendezvous.

"Broadway's always busy," Drake said. "Let's do Eighth."

Alicia stared at him. "How the hell would you know?"

"I've heard of Broadway. Never heard of Eighth."

"Oh, fair enough. Where—"

"No! It is Broadway!" Beau abruptly cried in his almost musical accent. "Restaurant is at the top . . . almost."

"Almost?"

"With me!"

Beau set off like a hundred meter sprinter, vaulting a parked car almost as if it wasn't there. Drake, Alicia and Mai stayed hot on his heels, turning east towards

Broadway and the intersection where Times Square shimmered and shone and flouted its flickering displays.

Again the crowds were difficult to part and again, Beau led them along the side of the road. Even here, tourists congregated, leaning back to scrutinize lofty buildings and billboards or trying to decide whether to play chicken with their lives and dash across the busy road. Touts worked the crowds, offering cheap tickets to various Broadway shows. Languages of every color filled the air, an almost overwhelming, complicated medley. The homeless weren't many, but those who advocated for them campaigned very loudly and forcefully for donations.

Ahead, Broadway thronged with New York's citizens and visitors, dotted by crosswalks, bordered by colorful shops and restaurants with their hanging, illuminated signs and A-board displays. Passersby were a blur as Drake and his section of the SPEAR team raced on.

Fifteen minutes.

Beau stared back at him. "Nav says it's a twenty two minute walk, but the sidewalks are so packed everyone's walking at the same pace."

"Then run," Alicia urged him. "Waggle that enormous tail of yours. Maybe it will make you go faster."

Before Beau could say anything, Drake felt his already plummeting heart sink even further. The road ahead was entirely blocked, both ways, and mostly by yellow cabs. A fender bender had occurred and those who weren't trying to drive around it were inching their vehicles out for a better look. The sidewalk to either side was a crush of humanity.

"Bloody hell."

But Beau didn't even break stride. An easy leap took him onto the trunk of the nearest cab and then he was running across its roof, jumping down to the hood and taking a running leap onto the next in line. Mai followed fast, and then Alicia, leaving Drake at the back to be shouted at and targeted by the vehicles' owners.

Drake was forced to concentrate beyond the norm. These cars weren't all the same, and their metals shifted, some were even rolling slowly forward. The race was hairy, but they leapt from vehicle to vehicle, using the long line to make headway. Crowds stared from either side. The good thing was they were unobstructed up here, and able to see the approaching intersection of Broadway and 54th, then 57th. As the crush of cars eased out, Beau rolled off the last car and resumed his sprint along the road itself, Mai at his side. Alicia glanced back at Drake.

"Just checking you didn't fall through that open sunroof back there."

"Yeah, dicey one that. I'm just thankful there were no convertibles."

Past another crossroads and 57th was lined with concrete mixer trucks, delivery vans and red and white barriers. If the team had thought they'd gained ground, or that this run would be as straight forward as the last, their illusions were abruptly shattered.

Two men appeared around the side of a delivery truck, handguns pointed straight at the runners. Drake didn't miss a beat. Constant battle, years of combat, had honed his senses to the max and kept them there—twenty four hours a day. The threatening forms registered immediately and, without hesitation, he flung himself headlong on top of them, right in front of the oncoming cement truck. One of the guns rattled away and the other became stuck under one of the men's bodies. Drake reeled back as a punch battered the side of his skull. Behind them, he heard the screech of the cement truck's wheels as it braked hard, the cursing of its driver . . .

Saw the enormous gray body swinging around towards him . . .

And heard Alicia's terrified scream.

"Matt!"

CHAPTER NINE

Drake could only watch as the out-of-control truck veered toward him. His attackers didn't even let up for a second, raining blows down because their own safety wasn't a concern to them. He took a fist to the throat, the chest and the solar plexus. He watched the swinging body, and kicked out as it swung right over his head.

The first terrorist fell backward, stumbling away, and was struck by one of the wheels, the impact breaking his back and ending his threat. The second blinked as if stunned by Drake's effrontery, then turned his head toward the approaching body of the truck.

The wet slapping sound was enough. Drake knew he was out of it, and then saw the first terrorist's skull chewed beneath the sliding wheels as the truck's body slewed around above him. Frame flattened, he could only hope. Darkness blotted out everything, even sound for a split second. The underside of the truck moved over him, slowing, slowing, and then came to an abrupt stop.

Alicia's hand reached underneath. "You okay?"

Drake rolled towards her. "Better than those guys."

Beau was waiting, almost hopping from foot to foot as he checked his own watch. "Four minutes left!"

Aching, bruised, scraped and battered, Drake

forced his body into action. Alicia stayed with him this time, as if sensing he might be a little distracted after the near miss. They weaved around the tourist gangs, finding Central Park South and the Marea among a host of other restaurants.

Mai pointed it out, the signage comparatively discreet for New York City.

Beau ran ahead. Drake and the others caught him up at the door. A waitress stared at them and their disheveled appearance, their heavy jackets, and backed away. Her eyes showed that she'd seen damage and suffering before.

"Don't worry," Drake said. "We're the English."

Mai sent a glare his way. "Japanese."

And Beau interrupted his search for the men's room with a raised eyebrow. "Definitely not English."

Drake ran as gracefully as he could through the still-closed restaurant, clipping a chair and table as he went. The men's restroom was small, consisting of only two urinals and a toilet. He checked under the bowl.

"Nothing here," he said.

Stress crisscrossed Beauregard's face. He tapped the buttons of his watch. "Time's up."

The hovering waitress jumped as the telephone rang. Drake held out a hand to her. "Take your time. Please, take your time."

He thought she might bolt, but inner resolve sent her toward the receiver. At that moment Alicia came out of the female restroom, a fraught expression on her face. "It's not there. We don't have it!"

Drake flinched as if he'd been struck. He stared around. Could there be another restroom in this tiny restaurant? An employee's stall perhaps? They would have to check again, but the waitress was already speaking on the phone. Her eyes flickered toward Drake and she told the caller to hold.

"It's a man called Marsh. For you."

Drake frowned. "Did he ask for me by name?"

"An Englishman, he said." The waitress shrugged. "That's all he said."

Beau lingered at his side. "And since you are easily confused, my friend, that is you."

"Cheers."

Drake reached out for the phone, one hand rubbing the side of his face as a rush of weariness and tension washed over him. How could they fail now? They had defeated all the odds and yet Marsh might still somehow be playing them.

"Yes?"

"Marsh here. Now tell me, what did you find?"

Drake opened his mouth, then closed it quickly. What was the right answer? Maybe Marsh was expecting the word "nothing". Maybe . . .

He paused, wavering from reply to reply.

"Tell me what you found or I will give the order to kill two New Yorkers within the next minute."

Drake opened his mouth. Dammit! "We found—"

Then Mai came sprinting out of the women's rest room, slipping on the wet tiles and falling onto her side. In her hand was clasped a small white envelope. Beau was next to her in a split-second, retrieving the envelope and handing it to Drake. Mai languished on the floor, panting hard.

Alicia stared open-mouthed at her. "Where did you find that, Sprite?"

"You did what they call a 'boy look', Taz. And that shouldn't surprise anyone, since you're three-quarters male anyway."

Alicia fumed in silence.

Drake was coughing as he tore open the envelope. "We . . . found . . . a . . . a bloody USB stick, Marsh. Shit, man, what is this?"

"Well done. Well done. I'm a little disappointed but, hey, maybe next time. Now just take a good look at the USB. This is your final verification and, as before, you may want to pass it on to someone with a bigger brain than yourselves or the NYPD."

"Is it the inside of the . . . cake?" Drake was aware of the waitress still standing nearby.

Marsh laughed loudly. "Oh good, oh very good. Let's not let the cat out of the bag, eh? Yes, it is. Now listen, I will give you ten minutes to send the USB's contents to your betters, and then we start again."

"No, no we don't." Drake waved toward Mai, who carried a small backpack in which they had stashed a tiny laptop. The Japanese woman dragged herself off the ground and came over.

"We won't chase our tails all over this city, Marsh."

"Umm, yes you will. Because I say so. Now, time is ticking. Let's get that laptop booted up and enjoy what happens next, shall we? Five, four . . ."

Drake smashed a fist into a table as the line went

quiet. Anger boiled his blood. "Listen, Marsh—"

The restaurant's front window exploded as the front fender of a van smashed through into the eating area. Glass shattered and tore slices from the air. Woodwork, plastic and mortar burst into the room. The van didn't stop, crashing down onto its tires and roaring like death's apprentice as it tore through the small room.

CHAPTER TEN

Julian Marsh felt a sharp pain in his stomach as he rolled to the right. Slices of pizza fell to the floor and a bowl of salad tumbled across the sofa. Quickly he clutched his sides, quite unable to stop laughing.

The low-slung table that sat before Zoe and him juddered as a wild foot gave it an errant kick. Zoe reached out a hand to steady him, patting his shoulder rapidly as another exciting event began to unfold. So far, they had watched Drake and his team spill out of the Edison—viewing quite easily as they had a man dressed as a tourist filming the event from across the street—then seen the mad dash up Broadway—this hysterical tableau more sporadic as there were only so many traffic and security cams a local terrorist could hack into—and then viewed with bated breath the attack that had somehow evolved around the concrete mixer.

All a nice distraction. Marsh had held a burner cell in one hand and Zoe's thigh in the other, whilst she scarfed down several slices of ham and mushroom and messed around on Facebook.

Three screens, eighteen-inch each, faced them. The pair now exhibited rapt attention as Drake and Co. stormed into the little Italian restaurant. Marsh checked the time and glanced at the colorful façade.

"Shit, this is a close one."

"Are you excited?"

"Yeah, aren't you?"

"It's an okay movie." Zoe pouted. "But I was hoping for more blood."

"Just give it a minute, my love. It gets better."

The pair sat and played in a rented apartment that belonged to one of the terrorist cells; the primary one, Marsh thought. There were four terrorists, one of whom had set up the cinema-like viewing area for Marsh by previous request. Whilst the Pythian couple enjoyed their viewing pleasure the men sat aside, crowded around a small TV, and monitored dozens of other channels, searching for tidbits of news or awaiting a call of some sort. Marsh didn't know and didn't give a hoot. He also ignored the odd looks and stolen glances, knowing full well that he was a good-looking man, with a quirky personality, and some people—even other men—liked to appreciate such individuality.

Zoe showed him a little more appreciation, slipping her hands down the front of his boxers. Damn, but her nails were sharp.

Sharp and yet somehow . . . pleasurable.

He spent a moment gazing at the suitcase nuke, a term he couldn't quite remove from his mind even though the minimized bomb sat in a large backpack, and then shoveled a little caviar into his mouth. The spread before them was magnificent, of course, comprised of foods priceless and tawdry, but all delicious.

Was that the nuke calling his name?

Marsh saw that it was time to act and made the call, speaking to a charming waitress and then the thick-accented Englishman. The guy had one of those bizarre tones of voices—something smacking of peasantry—and Marsh made twisted faces as he tried to decipher vowel from vowel. Not an easy task, and made somewhat harder with a woman's hands squeezing your nutcracker suite.

"Tell me what you found or I will give the order to kill two New Yorkers within the next minute." Marsh grinned as he said it, ignoring the annoyed looks cast by his disciples across the room.

The Englishman hesitated some more. Marsh found a slice of cucumber fallen out of the salad bowl and stuck it deep into Zoe's hair. Not that she'd ever notice. Minutes passed and Marsh conversed over the burner cell, becoming more and more excited. A cold bottle of Bollinger sat nearby and he spent half a minute pouring a large glass. Zoe snuggled up to him as she worked, and they sipped from the same glass, opposite rims of course.

"Five," Marsh said into the phone. "Four, three . . ."

Zoe's hands took on a particular urgency.

"Two."

The Englishman tried to barter with him, clearly wondering what the hell was going on. Marsh imagined the vehicle he'd arranged to be plowed through the front window at a pre-determined time, aiming now, accelerating, bearing down on the unsuspecting restaurant.

"One."

And then everything exploded.

CHAPTER ELEVEN

Drake flung his body toward the restaurant wall, grabbing the waitress around the waist and taking her with him. Glass and brick fragments sluiced off his rolling body. The oncoming van squealed for traction as its tires struck the restaurant floor and its middle rocked over the window sill, its back end now rising and smashing into the lintel above the pane. Metal screeched. Tables collapsed. Chairs piled up as debris before it.

Alicia had also reacted instantly, scrambling around a table and away, her only wound a small gash across the shin from a fast-moving splinter of wood. Mai somehow managed to roll across the top of a moving table, escaping any harm and Beau went one better, leaping above her and jumping from surface to surface, at last timing a jump so that his feet and hands struck the side wall and helped him land safely.

Drake looked up, the waitress screaming at his side. Alicia stared accusingly.

"So you grabbed her, did you?"

"Look out!"

The van still came forward, slowing by the second, but now the barrel of a gun poked out of the lowered passenger window. Alicia ducked and covered. Mai rolled some more. Drake withdrew his own handgun and fired six bullets at the disembodied hand, the sounds loud in the confined space, vying with the van's deafening roar. Beau was already in motion, darting around the back of the vehicle. At last the wheels stopped turning and ground to a halt. Broken tables and chairs cascaded from the hood and even from the roof. Drake made sure the waitress was unharmed before moving forward, but by then Beau and Mai were already at the vehicle.

Beau had smashed the driver's window and was grappling with a figure. Mai checked positioning through the smashed windshield and then picked up a splintered length of wood.

"No," Drake began, his voice a little croaky. "We need—"

But Mai wasn't in the mood for listening. Instead she threw the improvised weapon through the windshield with enough force that it stuck hard in the driver's forehead, quivering in place. The man's eyes rolled up and he stopped struggling with Beau, the Frenchman looking bemused.

"I did have him."

Mai shrugged. "I thought I should help."

"Help?" Drake repeated. "We need at least one of these bastards alive."

"And on that note," Alicia piped up. "I'm fine, ta. Nice to see you saving Waitress Wendy's ass though."

Drake bit his tongue, knowing at some deep level that Alicia was only ribbing him. Beauregard had already dragged the driver out of the vehicle and was rifling his pockets. Alicia headed over to the miraculously untouched laptop. The USB had finished uploading and had deposited a hash of pictures onto the screen—disturbing images of silver canisters that made Drake's blood run cold.

"It appears to be the inside of a bomb," he said, studying wires and relays. "Send it to Moore before anything else happens."

Alicia leaned over the machine, tapping away.

Drake helped the waitress to her feet. "You okay, love?"

"I . . . I think so."

"Mint. Now how about rustling us up a lasagna?"

"The chef . . . the chef hasn't arrived yet." Her gaze swept the destruction fearfully.

"Hell, and I thought you just threw 'em into a microwave."

"Don't worry." Mai came over and laid a hand on the waitress's arm. "They will remodel. Insurance should take care of this."

"I hope so."

Drake again bit his tongue, this time to stop a curse. Yes, it was a blessing that everyone was still breathing but Marsh and his cronies were still wrecking people's lives. Without conscience. Without ethics and without concern.

As if by psychic link the phone rang. This time Drake picked it up.

"Are you all still kicking?"

Marsh's voice made him want to hit something, but he kept it strictly professional. "We've forwarded your pictures on."

"Oh, excellent. So that's that bit sorted out then. I

hope you grabbed a bite to eat whilst you waited because this next part—well, it could kill you."

Drake coughed. "You do know we haven't verified your bomb yet."

"And, hearing that, I see that you want to slow events down whilst you try to catch up. Not happening, my new friend. Not happening at all. Your cops and agents, military people and fire department, may be part of a well-oiled machine, but they are still a machine, and take a little while to get up to speed. Therefore, I take that time to tear you apart. It's quite fun, believe me."

"What do the Pythians get out of all this?"

Marsh clucked. "Oh, I think you know that conceited group of ragamuffins recently imploded. Was anything ever more certain? They were led by a serial killer, a psycho stalker, a megalomaniac and a jealous domineer. All of whom happened to be the same person."

Alicia leaned closer to Drake at that moment. "So tell us—where is that bastard?"

"Oh, a new girl. Are you the blonde or the Asian? Probably the blonde by the sound of it. Darling, if I knew where he was I'd let you flay him alive. Tyler Webb only ever wanted one thing. He abandoned the Pythians the moment he knew where to find it."

"Which was at the bazaar?" Drake asked, now playing both for time and information.

"A hive of heinousness that place, am I right? Imagine all the deals done there that will impact the world for decades to come."

"Ramses sold him something," Drake said, testing.

"Yes. And I'm sure the tricky French Pain Au Sausage has already told you what that item was. Or you could always ask him right now."

So that confirmed it. Marsh was watching them, though he didn't have eyes in the restaurant. Drake sent a quick text to Moore. "How about telling us where Webb went?"

"Well, seriously, what am I, Fox News? You'll be asking me for cash next."

"I'll settle for that terrorist asshole."

"And back to the job at hand." Marsh spoke the words and then seemed amused at himself, abruptly laughing. "Sorry, private joke. But we're done now with the verification part of the chase. Now I want to give you my demands."

"So just tell us." Alicia sounded weary.

"Where's the fun in that? This bomb will detonate unless I am completely satisfied. Who knows, dear, I may have even chosen to own you."

In an instant, Alicia appeared ready to go, eyes and expression so fired up she could ignite a desiccated forest.

"I'd love to get you alone," she whispered.

Marsh paused, then continued quickly. "The Natural History Museum, twenty minutes."

Drake set his watch. "And then?"

"Hmmm, what?"

"It's a big ass piece of architecture."

"Oh, well if you get that far I'd suggest stripping a male guard called Jose Gonzales. One of our associates sewed my demands into the lining of his jacket last night. Ingenious way to transport documents, eh, and with no comeback to the originator."

Drake didn't reply, more perplexed than anything.

"I know what you're thinking," Marsh said, again showing amazing cerebral qualities. "Why not just mail you the pics and tell you my demands? Well, I am a peculiar man. They told me I have two sides, two minds and two faces, but I prefer to see it as two separate qualities. One part twisted, the other bent. You see what I mean?"

Drake coughed. "I certainly know what you are."

"Excellent, then I know you will understand that when I see your four torn-apart corpses in about seventeen minutes, I will feel both wonderfully happy and terribly annoyed. With you. Now, goodbye."

The line went dead. Drake clicked his watch.

Twenty minutes.

CHAPTER TWELVE

Hayden and Kinimaka spent their time with Ramses. The terrorist prince appeared ill at ease in his six-foot square cell: dirty, disheveled and, though clearly exhausted, pacing like a caged lion. Hayden donned a flak jacket, checked her Glock and spare ammo, and bade Mano do the same. No chances would be taken from here on in. Both Ramses and Marsh had proven too clever to underestimate.

Perhaps the terrorist myth was right where he wanted to be.

Hayden doubted it, doubted it immensely. The fight inside the castle and the desperate death of his bodyguard had showed how anxious he'd been to escape. Also, was his reputation ruined? Shouldn't he be trying desperately to repair the damage? Probably, but the man wasn't destroyed to the level where he couldn't rebuild. Hayden watched him stride as Kinimaka fetched them a couple of plastic chairs.

"There is a nuclear weapon in this city," Hayden said. "Which I am sure you know, since you brokered the deal to Tyler Webb and Julian Marsh. You are in this city and if the time comes we'll make damn sure you're not underground. Of course, your followers don't know we have you . . ." She let it hang right there.

Ramses pulled up, tired eyes fixing on her. "You

refer to the double-cross of course, where my men will soon kill Marsh, take charge of the bomb and detonate. You must know this through Webb and his bodyguard since they are the only ones who knew. And you also know that they merely await my command." He nodded as if to himself.

Hayden waited. Ramses was sharp, but that didn't mean he wouldn't slip up.

"They will detonate," Ramses said. "They will make the decision themselves."

"We can make your last few hours pretty much intolerable," Kinimaka said.

"You won't make me call it off," Ramses said. "Even through torture. I will not halt that detonation."

"What do you want?" Hayden asked.

"There will be negotiation."

She studied him, looking intently into the face of the new world enemy. These people didn't want anything in return, they wouldn't negotiate and they believed death was but a step up to some kind of Heaven. *Where does that leave us?*

Where indeed? She felt for her weapon. "A man who wants nothing other than to commit mass murder is easily dealt with," she said. "With a bullet to the head."

Ramses pressed his face to the bars. "Then go ahead, western bitch."

Hayden didn't need to be an expert to read the madness and zeal shining from those soul-dead eyes. Without a word she changed tack and exited the room, locking the outer door carefully behind her.

Never too careful.

The next room along housed the cell of Robert Price. She had gained permission to keep the Secretary here because of the imminent threat and his potential part in it. As she and Kinimaka walked into the room, Price turned a supercilious expression upon her.

"What do you know about the bomb?" she said. "And why were you in the Amazon, attending a terrorist bazaar?"

Price sank down into his bunk. "I want a lawyer. And what do you mean? A bomb?"

"Nuclear bomb," Hayden said. "Here in New York. Help yourself, you piece of shit. Help yourself right now by telling us what you know."

"Seriously." Price stared. "I know nothing."

"You committed treason," Kinimaka said, moving his bulk close to the cell. "Is that how you want to be remembered? An epitaph for your grandkids. Or would you rather be known as the repentant who helped save New York?"

"As lovely as you make that sound," Price's voice rattled like a coiled snake. "I wasn't involved in any 'bomb' negotiations and know nothing. Now, please, my lawyer."

"I'll give you a little while," Hayden said. "Then I'm gonna put Ramses and you together, in the same cell. You can fight it out. We'll see who talks first. He would rather die, not live, and he wants to take every living soul with him. You? Just make sure you don't commit suicide."

Price looked flustered at at-least some of her words. "No lawyer?"

Hayden turned around. "Fuck you."

The Secretary watched her go. Hayden locked him inside and then turned to Mano. "Any ideas?"

"I'm wondering if Webb is involved in this. He's been the figurehead all along."

"Not this time, Mano. Webb isn't even stalking us anymore. This is all Ramses and Marsh, I'm sure."

"So what's next?"

"I don't know how else we can help Drake and the guys," Hayden said. "The team is already at the very core of this. Homeland have everything else managed, from cops kicking in doors to spies pulling their hard-earned covers, to army build-up and the arrival of NEST, the Nuclear Emergency Support Team. FDNY are everywhere, with all they've got. The bomb squad is at the highest alert. We have to find a way to break Ramses."

"You saw him. How do you break a man who doesn't care if he lives or dies?"

Hayden stopped angrily. "We have to try. Or would you rather just give up? Everyone has a trigger. That worm cares for something. His fortune, his lifestyle, a concealed family? There has to be something we can do to help."

Kinimaka wished they could call on Karin Blake's computer expertise, but the woman was still embroiled in her Fort Bragg regime. "Let's go find a workstation."

"And pray we have time."

"They're waiting for Ramses' go ahead. We have some time."

"You heard him as well as I, Mano. Sooner or later, they're gonna kill Marsh and detonate."

CHAPTER THIRTEEN

Dahl listened to the conflicting comms reports as Smyth guided their vehicle through the congested streets of Manhattan. Luckily, they didn't have far to go and not every concrete artery was fully clogged. The entire cast of informers had been dragged out for this one, it seemed, from the lowliest gutter snitch to the richest, dishonest billionaire and everything in between. This made for a clutter of conflicting reports, but Homeland were doing their very best to sort the reliable from the polluted.

"Two of the known cells have strong links to a nearby mosque," Moore was telling Dahl over the earpiece. He reeled off an address. "We have an undercover there, though he's pretty new. Says the place has been on lockdown all day."

Dahl was never a man to assume anything. "What does that actually mean in mosque terminology?"

"What does it mean? It means get the hell in there and flush out at least one of Ramses' cells."

"Civilian activity?"

"Nothing much to speak of. But whoever is in there ain't likely saying prayers. Search all the back rooms and underground chambers. And gear up. My guy's not often wrong, and I trust his gut on this one."

Dahl relayed the information and punched the coordinates into the GPS. As luck had it they were almost on top of the mosque and Smyth wrenched the wheel towards the curb.

"Providence," Lauren said.

"The name I gave my old katana." Kenzie sighed in memory.

Dahl tightened the buckles of his vest. "We ready? Same formation. We hit hard and fast, people. No quarter."

Smyth switched the engine off. "No problem with me."

Morning still greeted them as they climbed out and studied the mosque across the road. A red and white vent stood nearby, billowing steam. Situated at a junction, the building ran along the sides of both streets, its colorful windows and extended frontage a part of the community. Atop the building sat a small minaret, odd and almost flashy against the surrounding concrete facades. The off-street entry was through a pair of glass doors.

"We walk in," Dahl said. "Now move."

They headed across the road with hard purpose, stopping traffic with outstretched hands. A pause now could cost them everything.

"Big place," Smyth commented. "Hard to find a determined group inside there."

Dahl contacted Moore. "We're on site. Do you have anything else for us?"

"Yeah. My man assures me the cell meets underground. He's close to being accepted, but not close enough to help us today."

Dahl relayed the news as they crossed the other

sidewalk and pushed on the front doors of the mosque. With senses hyper-aware they inched inside, eyes adjusting to the slightly dimmer light. White walls and ceiling glared back, along with gold light fittings and a red and gold carpet, decorated with patterns. This all nestled beyond a reception area, where a man eyed them with open suspicion.

"Can I help you?"

Dahl produced his SPEAR ID. "Yes, my man, you can. You can lead us to your secret underground entrance."

The receptionist appeared nonplussed. "Is this a joke?"

"Move aside," Dahl held out a hand.

"Hey, I can't let you—"

Dahl picked the man up by the front of his shirt and set him on top of the counter. "I believe I said—move aside."

The team hurried past and into the main body of the mosque. The area was empty and the doors at the back locked. Dahl waited for cover from Smyth and Kenzie and then kicked them twice. Wood splintered and panels fell to the floor. At that moment there came noises and the sounds of scuffling from the foyer behind. The team fell into position, covering the area. Three seconds passed and then the face and helmet of a SWAT commander popped around the sidewall.

"You Dahl?"

The Swede grunted. "Yes?"

"Moore sent us. SWAT. We're here to back your play."

"Our play?"

"Yeah. New Intel. You're in the wrong friggin' mosque, and they're dug in pretty deep. It's gonna take a frontal assault to swill 'em out. And we're aiming for legs."

Dahl didn't like it, but understood the procedure, the etiquettes of operating here. And it didn't hurt that SWAT already had a better location.

"Lead the way," Dahl said.

"We are. The correct mosque is across the street."

"Across the . . ." Dahl cursed. "Bloody GPS bollocks."

"They're quite close together." The officer shrugged. "And that English cursing is heartwarming, but shall we get our friggin' asses moving?"

Minutes ticked by as the teams mingled and formed a raiding party as they re-crossed the road. Once assembled not another moment was wasted. A full-scale assault began. Men attacked the front of the building, battering the doors and spilling into the foyer. A second wave passed through them, fanning out and searching for reference points they had been told of. Once a blue door was found, a man positioned an explosive charge against it and detonated. An explosion radiated out, the blast much wider than Dahl expected, but of a radius SWAT had clearly planned for.

"Booby trapped," the leader told him. "There will be more."

The Swede breathed a little easier, already knowing the value of undercover agents and now remembering to pay tribute to them. Undercover was among the most treacherous and life-changing of all police methods. It was a rare and valuable asset who could infiltrate the enemy and thus save lives.

SWAT eased inside a mostly destroyed room, then angled toward a far door. This stood open and covered what was clearly the entrance to a cellar. As the first man approached gunfire sounded from below and a bullet ricocheted through the room.

Dahl glanced at Kenzie. "Any ideas?"

"You're asking me? Why?"

"Maybe because I picture you having a room like this of your own."

"Don't beat around the fucking bush, Dahl, will you? I am not your pet smuggler. I am here only because . . . because—"

"Yes, why are you here?"

"I really wish I knew. Maybe I should go . . ." She hesitated, then sighed. "Look, maybe there's another way inside. A clever criminal wouldn't go down there without a solid escape route. But with actual terrorist cells? Who knows with such suicidal bastards?"

"We don't have dithering time," the SWAT leader said, crouching nearby. "It's rollerball for these guys."

Dahl watched the team take out stun grenades even as he considered Kenzie's words. Purposely harsh, he believed they hid a caring heart, or at least the shattered vestiges of one. Kenzie needed something to help piece those parts back together—but how long could she search without losing all hope? That ship might already be wrecked.

SWAT signaled they were ready and then unleashed a crazy form of hell by way of the wooden stairwell. As the grenades bounced down and then burst the teams stepped forward, Dahl jostling the commander for pole position.

Smyth squeezed past. "Move your asses."

Running downwards they were instantly met with gunfire. Dahl caught a glimpse of a dirt floor, table legs and crates of weapons before he deliberately slithered down four risers in a row, gun out, returning fire. Smyth twisted before him, rolling to the bottom and crawling to the side. The SWAT team pounded behind, crouching and unflinching in the line of fire. Bullets were returned shot for shot, deadly salvos lacing the basement and taking chunks out of the thick walls. When Dahl hit the dirt at the bottom he immediately evaluated the scenario.

Four cell members were down here, which gelled with what they had seen of the previous cell. Three were on their knees, ears bleeding, hands held to their foreheads, whilst the fourth appeared unaffected and fired hard at his attackers. Perhaps the other three had shielded him, but Dahl instantly picked out a way of gaining a live captive and sighted on the shooter.

"Oh no!" The SWAT leader inexplicably burst past him.

"Hey!" Dahl called. "What—"

In the midst of the worst kind of hell only those who have experienced it before can act without pause. The SWAT leader had clearly spotted a sign, something recognizable to him, and considered only the lives of his colleagues. As Dahl squeezed his own trigger he saw the terrorist drop a primed grenade from one hand and throw down his weapon with the other.

"For Ramses!" he cried.

The cellar was a death-trap, a small room to where these creatures had lured their prey. Other traps lay about the room, traps that would be triggered by a shrapnel explosion. Dahl shot the terrorist between the eyes even as he knew the gesture was merely academic—it would not save them.

Not inside this tiny brick-walled room, crowded together, as the last seconds ticked away before the grenade exploded.

CHAPTER FOURTEEN

Dahl saw the world go dark. He saw time slow to crawling pace, the beat of every living heart measured in endless moments. When the grenade bounced, displacing dust and dirt from the floor in a tiny mushroom cloud, his bullet entered the terrorist's skull, clattering around before it burst out of the back and struck the wall amidst a wide fountain of blood. The body slackened, the life already departed. The grenade came down for its second bounce and Dahl started to let the gun fall away from his face.

Precious seconds remained.

Three terrorists were still on their knees, groaning and defeated, and they did not see what was coming. SWAT guys were trying to arrest their momentum or scramble back up the steps.

Smyth was turning his gaze up at Dahl, the last vision of his life.

Dahl knew that Kenzie and Lauren and Yorgi were at the top of the stairs and had half a moment of hope they were far enough away from the epicenter.

And still, this is all for my children . . .

The grenade exploded at the height of its second bounce, the sound momentarily the loudest thing the Swede had ever heard. Then all sound was suddenly smothered as thought fell away . . .

His eyes were fixed ahead, and couldn't believe what they were seeing.

The SWAT leader had sprinted with everything he had, knowing what was coming and determined to save as many as he could, realizing instantly that he was the only person who could do so. His run took him above the grenade, enabling him to fall directly on top of it in the split-second before it erupted. Through Kevlar and flesh and bone it detonated, but did not touch those who stood transfixed about the room. The blast was muffled and then was gone.

Dahl cleared his throat, unable to believe his own eyes. The selflessness of his colleagues always humbled him, but this was on another level.

I didn't . . . I didn't even know his name.

And still, terrorists knelt before him.

Dahl raced down the last few steps, tears blinding his eyes even as he kicked the three men onto their backs. Smyth tore their jackets open. No explosive vests were apparent, but one man started to foam at the mouth even as Smyth knelt by his side. Another writhed in agony. The third was pinned down, immobile. Dahl met the man's terrible, polar-cap gaze with a hatred of his own. Kenzie came up and caught the Swede's attention, looking at Dahl, her ice-blue eyes so clear and cold and flooded with feeling they appeared to be a vast, thawing landscape, and mouthed the only words she could muster.

"He saved us by sacrificing himself. I . . . I feel so deficient, so deplorable, compared to him."

Dahl, in all his days, had never found himself unable to comment. He did now.

Smyth frisked all three men, coming up with more

grenades, bullets and small arms. Papers and notes were crumpled in pockets, so the assembled men started to rummage through them.

Others walked over to their fallen leader, heads bowed. One man knelt and reached out a hand to touch the officer's back.

The third terrorist died, whatever poison he had consumed simply taking longer to act than his colleagues'. Dahl watched dispassionately. When his earpiece squawked and Moore's voice filled his head he listened but could think of no answer.

"Five cells," Moore told him. "Our sources have found that Ramses has five cells in total. You've encountered two, which leaves three remaining. Do you have any new information for me, Dahl? Hello? You there? What the hell is happening?"

The mad Swede toggled a small button that would turn Moore mute. He wanted at least a few seconds to pay his respects in silence. Like all the men and women down there, he survived only because of one man's enormous sacrifice. This man would never see the light of day again nor the setting sun, or feel a warm breeze play upon on his face. Dahl would experience that for him.

For as long as he lived.

CHAPTER FIFTEEN

Seventeen minutes.

Drake followed Beau's lead, cutting left down 59th and heading straight into the chaos that was Columbus Circle. Flags fluttered from buildings to his left, a green swathe lay to his right, sprinkled with trees. A mostly glass apartment building sat up ahead, its windows glinting in welcome to the still rising sun. A yellow cab slowed at the curb, its driver expectant on seeing four heavily clothed sprinters hightailing it along the sidewalk, but Beau didn't give the man a second glance. The circle was a wide, concrete expanse with waterfalls and statues and places to sit. Tourists wandered to and fro, repacking rucksacks and drinking water. Drake drilled through the middle of a group of sweating athletes, then ran under a stretch of trees that offered at least a little shadow.

Out of sight of prying eyes.

The contrast of the austere, hectic streets with their many extremes – the majestic, cluttered skyscrapers vying for space among traditional churches along a uniform grid system – and the utter peace and calm that inhabited the greenery off to his right filled Drake with a sense of unreality. How crazy was this place? How dreamlike? The distinctions were unimaginably extreme.

He wondered just how closely Marsh was watching

them, but didn't mind too much. It could be the undoing of the man. Homeland were even now trying to find the feed so they could trace it back to a source.

A flamboyant globe spun slowly to the left as the group sped on. Alicia and Mai ran close behind, keeping watch but unable to use their full abilities at this kind of pace. The enemy could be anywhere, anyone. A passing sedan with blacked out windows warranted a closer inspection, but vanished into the distance.

Drake checked the time. Eleven minutes left.

And still the moments ticked away, second after second. Beau slowed as a light gray building appeared over the road, one Drake instantly recognized. Still running, he turned to Alicia and Mai. "Same building we fought in during the Odin thing. Shit, seems like a lifetime ago now."

"Didn't a helicopter hit the side?" Alicia asked.

"Oh yeah, and a T. Rex attacked us."

The Natural History Museum appeared comparatively small from this angle, a misconception if ever there was one. Steps rose from the sidewalk to the front doors, currently thronged by a group of tourists. The combined smells of diesel and petrol assaulted them as they stopped at the curb. The noise of engines, honking horns and random shouting still tattered their senses, but at least the traffic was moving past here.

"Don't stop now," Alicia said. "We have no idea where the guard will be."

Drake attempted to stop the traffic and allow them to cross. "Let's hope he didn't call in sick."

Luckily, the vehicle flow was light and the group managed to thread their way across the road quite easily. Once at the base of the museum's steps they started up, all coming to a sudden halt as they heard the loud screech of tires behind them.

Drake thought: *Seven minutes.*

They turned to a scene of unreserved madness. Four men jumped out of a car, rifles held in the air. Drake scrambled to evade, leaping away from the museum's doors and straggling visitors. Beau swiftly withdrew his own weapon and took a bead on the enemy. Shots were fired. Screams tore the morning to shreds.

Drake leapt high and hit low, rolling as he struck the sidewalk and ignoring the pain where his shoulder took the full force of his body. An assailant had leapt onto the hood of a sedan and was already lining Mai up in his sights. Drake rolled against the vehicle and then rose, fortunate to find himself within grabbing distance of the rifle. He reached up, becoming the clearer threat and demanding attention.

Alicia dived the other way, clearing the steps and putting the Equestrian Statue of Theodore Roosevelt between her and her attackers. Still, they fired, bullets hammering into the bronze molding. Alicia drew her weapon and sneaked around the other side. Two men were now on top of cars, making nice targets. Civilians ran every which way, clearing the area. She took a bead on a terrorist who dropped to his knees but the constant thread of his fire swung towards her, forcing her to take cover.

Mai and Beau pressed themselves into a small indented arch near the museum's front entrance, squeezing tight to escape the flow of bullets that stitched their way across the stonework. Beau was facing the wall, unable to move, but Mai was looking out, her back to the Frenchman's.

"This is . . . awkward," Beauregard complained.

"And very fortunate that you are reed thin," Mai returned. She popped her head out and let loose a salvo. "You know, back when we first encountered you it seemed like you often fitted between the cracks in the walls."

"That would be useful right now."

"Like smoke." Mai leaned out again, returning fire. Bullets tacked a route above her head.

"Can we move?"

"Not unless you want to become perforated."

Drake gauged he didn't have time to bring his own weapon to bear, so tried to grab his adversary's. Too late he realized he couldn't quite reach it—the guy was too high up—and then he saw the yawning barrel turning his way.

Nowhere to go.

Instinct slammed through him like a projectile. Stepping back he kicked at the car window, smashing the glass and then dived through just as the terrorist opened fire. Behind him, the sidewalk churned. Drake squeezed through the gap and into the driver's seat, leather squeaking, the shape of the seats hampering his passage. He knew what was coming. A bullet smacked through the roof, the seat and the floor of the car. Drake shuffled faster. The central well was composed of a glove compartment and two large cup-holders, which gave him something to grip as he launched his bulk into the passenger seat. More bullets thunked mercilessly down through the roof. Drake cried out, playing for time. The flow stopped momentarily, but then as Drake leaned back and booted the window out it started again at an even faster rate.

Drake scrambled into the back seat, a bullet burning a graze down the center of his back. He ended up in an untidy heap, panting and out of ideas. His moment of delay must have made the shooter pause too, and then the man came under fire from Alicia. Drake unlocked the rear door from inside and slithered out, face-palming the concrete and seeing nowhere to go.

Except . . .

Under the car. He rolled, barely fitting under the vehicle. Now his vision was a black undercarriage, pipes and exhaust system. Another bullet fired down from above, slamming the gap between the open V of his legs. Drake exhaled, whistling in silence.

Two can play at this game.

One leg at a time, he forced his body along the ground and down to the front of the car, wrestling his Glock free as he went. Then, sighting up through previous bullet holes he approximated where the man would be. He fired six shots in succession, repositioning a little every time, and then quickly dragged himself out from under the car.

The terrorist fell down beside him, clutching his stomach. The rifle clattered down alongside him. As he reached desperately for it and also into his waistband, Drake shot him point blank. The risks were too great to gamble, the population too vulnerable. Aching muscles wracked him as he then struggled upright, peering over the hood of the car.

Alicia darted from around the Roosevelt statue, discharging several rounds before disappearing again. Her target was positioned on the front end of another car. Two more terrorists were trying to get an angle on Mai and Beau, who appeared to have somehow forced themselves into the wall, but Mai's accurate shooting was holding the terrorists back.

Drake checked his watch.

Two minutes.

They were well and truly fucked.

CHAPTER SIXTEEN

Drake took the battle to the terrorists. Unleashing his HK, he concentrated on the two who were worrying Beau and Mai. One fell instantly, his life spilled all over the concrete, a hard death for a hard-bitten heart. The other swiveled at the last moment, taking a bullet, but still able to return fire. Drake followed the man's roll with bullets, filling his wake with death. In the end the man had nowhere to go and stopped, then sat up and fired a final round toward Mai as Drake's gun ended his threat.

Mai saw it coming and pulled Beau to the floor. The Frenchman protested, landing in an ungainly heap, but Mai kept her elbows on top of him, preventing movement. Chunks burst from the wall right where their heads had been.

Beau stared upward. "Merci, Mai."

"Ki ni shinaide."

Drake by now had drawn the attention of the last remaining terrorist, but none of that mattered. Only the terrible fear in his soul mattered. Only the despairing pounding of his heart mattered.

They had missed the deadline.

His mood rose a little as he saw Mai and Beau race into the museum, and then Alicia stepped out of concealment to send the final terrorist to the raging hell he deserved. One more man bleeding on the sidewalk. One more soul lost and sacrificed.

They were endless, these people. They were the raging sea.

Drake then saw the last, supposedly dead, terrorist rise and stagger away. Drake figured he must have been wearing a vest. He sighted on the bobbing shoulders and fired, but the shot skimmed just millimeters above its target. Exhaling slowly he sighted in a second shot. Now the man fell to his knees and then rose again, and in the next instant he was barging into a crowd of people, looky loos, locals and kids with cameras all trying to grab their one minute of fame on Facebook or Instagram.

Drake staggered over to Alicia. "So that was one of Ramses' cells?"

"Four men. Just as Dahl described. This would be the third cell we've encountered as a team."

"And we still don't know Marsh's terms."

Alicia scanned the streets all around, the road and the stalled, abandoned cars. Then she whirled as Mai's shout caught their attention.

"We have the guard!"

Drake charged up the steps, head down, not even attempting to put his guns away. This was everything, this was their whole world. If Marsh rang they could—

Jose Gonzales held a cellphone out. "Are you the Englishman?"

Drake closed his eyes and put the device to his ear. "Marsh. You utter c—"

The Pythian's laughter cut him short. "Now, now, do not resort to banal profanities. Cursing is for the uneducated or so I am told. Or is it the other way around? But congratulations, my new friend, you are alive!"

"It'll take more than a few knobjobs to take us down."

"Oh, I'm sure. Would a nuke do it?"

Drake felt he could continue the infuriated rejoinders indefinitely but made a conscious effort to sew his mouth shut. Alicia, Mai and Beau crowded around the phone, and Jose Gonzales watched on with foreboding.

"Cat got your tongue? Oh and hey, why on earth didn't you answer Gonzales's phone?"

Drake bit his upper lip until the blood flowed. "I'm right here."

"Yes, yes, I can see that. But where were you . . . umm . . . four minutes ago?"

Drake remained silent.

"Poor old Jose was forced to answer his own phone. Didn't have a clue what I was babbling on about."

Drake attempted to divert Marsh. "We have the jacket. Where—"

"You're not listening to me, Englishman. You were late. Do you remember the penalty for being late?"

"Marsh. Stop fucking around. Do you want your demands met or not?"

"My demands? Well, of course they will be met, when I decide I'm good and ready. Now, you three be good little soldiers and wait right there. I'll just order up a couple of takeaways."

Drake cursed. "Don't do it. Don't you bloody do it!"

"Speak soon."

The line went dead. Drake stared into three pairs of haunted eyes and knew they were a mere reflection of his own. They had failed.

With a giant effort he managed to refrain from crushing the phone. Alicia took it upon herself to call in the imminent threat to Homeland. Mai made Gonzales shrug himself out of his jacket.

"Let's get on with it," she said. "We deal with what is before us and ready ourselves for what may come next."

Drake studied the horizons, the concrete and tree-lined ones, mind and heart far away and crushed at the very idea of Marsh's intentions. In the next few minutes innocents would die, and if he failed again there would be more.

"Marsh is going to detonate that bomb," he said. "Whatever he says. If we don't find it, the whole world will suffer. We're standing on the very edge . . ."

CHAPTER SEVENTEEN

Marsh laughed and hung up the phone with a flourish. Zoe cuddled in even further. "You sure showed him," she purred.

"Oh, yes, and now I'm going to show him even more."

Marsh plucked out yet another burner cell and checked the number he'd already saved to the memory. Convinced it was the right one he quickly dialed and waited. The voice that answered, all gruff and imposing, confirmed his expectations.

"You know what to do," he said.

"One? Or two?"

"Two, as we agreed. Then move on in case I need you again."

"Sure boss. I've been keeping up with events through my cellphone's app. Would sure have loved me some of that action."

Marsh huffed. "Are you a terrorist, Stephen?"

"Well, no I wouldn't put myself in that class. Not exactly."

"The do the job you've been paid to do. Right now."

Marsh flicked one of the screens to a city camera, just a mini-surveillance unit the neighboring businesses used to keep tabs on the comings and goings along the sidewalk. Stephen would cause havoc along this particular street and Marsh wanted to watch.

Zoe leaned across, trying to get a better view. "So what else are we going to do today?"

Marsh stared. "Isn't this enough for you? And you do suddenly seem a little soft, somewhat malleable, for a woman invited to join the big bad Pythians, Miss Zoe Sheers. Why is that? Is it because you like the mad in me?"

"I think so. And more than just a little. Maybe the champagne is going to my head."

"Good. Now shut up and watch."

The next few moments unfolded as Marsh wanted them to. Normal men and women would flinch at what they saw, even tough ones, but Marsh and Sheers viewed it with cold detachment. It then took Marsh only five minutes to save the footage and video-message it to the Englishman with the attached note: *Send this on to Homeland. I'll be in touch shortly.*

He wrapped Zoe up in one arm. Together they studied the chase's next scenario, which would have the Englishman and his three stooges actually knowing they would arrive too late before they even began. Superb. And the mayhem at the end . . . priceless.

Marsh remembered then that there were other people in the room. Ramses' primary cell and its members. They were sitting so quietly in a far corner of the apartment that he barely recalled their faces.

"Hey," he called. "The lady has run out of champagne. Would one of you drifter types be able to freshen her up?"

A man rose, his eyes filled with so much contempt

that Marsh squirmed. But the expression was quickly masked and became a fast bobbing of the head. "Sure can."

"Excellent. One more bottle should do it."

CHAPTER EIGHTEEN

Drake watched Mai rip open the guard's jacket as she searched for a list of demands. Alicia and Beau searched the gathering crowds, almost certain the last remaining member of the third cell would make some kind of move. Homeland were en route, only two minutes out. Sirens shrieked nearby as the cops gathered. Drake knew that by now the culminating incidents would have all New Yorkers on edge, and sightseers rattled. It might not be a bad thing if people stayed off the streets, but what more could the White House actually do?

Drones with radiation detectors were looping through the skies. Metal detectors were stopping everyone who merited attention and many who didn't. The Army and NEST were here. So many agents were roaming the streets it felt like a veteran's reunion. If Homeland, the FBI, CIA and NSA were doing their jobs correctly, then Marsh would surely be found.

Drake checked his watch. It was somewhat over an hour since this nightmare began.

Is that all?

Alicia nudged him. "She found something."

Drake watched as Mai removed a folded sheet of paper from Gonzales's ruined jacket.

The New Yorker winced at her and picked up a tattered sleeve in each hand. "Will the city give me comp . . . compen . . . compens—"

"The city can give you some advice," Alicia said dead-pan. "Next time use a little warm oil. Don't pay for bad company."

Gonzales shut up and slunk away.

Drake moved over to Mai. Marsh's demands had been printed on a white A4 sheet in what appeared to be the biggest typesetting. All in all, they were pretty straight forward.

"Five hundred million dollars," Mai read out. "And nothing else."

Beneath the demand was a sentence written in a contrasting small script.

"Details to follow shortly."

Drake knew exactly what that meant. "We're about to be sent on another wild goose chase."

Beauregard watched the crowds. "And we remain under surveillance, no doubt. It is certain this time that we will fail again."

Drake lost count of the cellphones being held up among the gathered throng, then heard the dull buzz of his cell's message tone and checked the screen. Even before he clicked onto the video link his scalp started to itch with deep foreboding. "Guys," he said and held the device at arm's length as they crowded around.

It was grainy and it was in black and white, but the camera was steady and clearly showed one of Drake's worst nightmares. "This is senseless," he said. "Killing people who have no idea what's going on. It's not for terror, it's not for gain. It's for . . ." He couldn't go on.

"Pleasure," Mai breathed. "We dig up more of these

bottom feeders every day. And the worst thing is, they dwell at the very heart of our communities."

Drake didn't waste another moment, but sent the link on to Homeland. The fact that Marsh appeared to be able to pluck his cellphone number out of the air wasn't particularly surprising given all he'd accomplished so far. The terrorists helping him were clearly more than expendable foot soldiers.

Drake watched the cops do their jobs. Alicia moved closer to him, then randomly pulled up the leg of her pants. "Y' see this?" she intoned. "Got this when you tried to kick my ass in the desert. And it's still bloody fresh. That's how fast this thing is moving along."

Drake took more than one impression from her words. There was the memory of their bonding, their new attraction; the inference to Mai and Beau that something had happened between them; and the more obvious reference to her own life so far—how fast it had been moving and how she was trying to slow things down.

In the direct line of fire.

"If we survive this," he said. "Team SPEAR is taking a week off."

"Torsty's already booked for Barbados," Alicia said.

"What happened in the desert?" Mai wondered.

Drake checked his watch, then his phone, overcome by an odd, surreal moment. Mounting upon the needless death and surging threat, upon the endless chase and the brutal battle, they were now kicking their heels and being forced to take several moment's respite. Of course, they needed the time to let go of the tension, the mounting anxiety that might eventually get them killed . . . but Alicia's way of doing it was always somewhat out of the box.

"Bikini. Beach. Blue waves," Alicia said. "That's me."

"Are you taking your new best friend?" Mai smiled. "Kenzie?"

"Y'know, Alicia, I don't think Dahl's booked a team holiday," Drake said, only half-joking. "More a family vacation."

Alicia growled. "What a bastard. We are family."

"Yes, but not in the way he wants. Y'know, Johanna and Dahl need a little time."

But Alicia was now staring hard at Mai. "And in answer to that initial jibe, Sprite, no, I was thinking of taking Drakey. That okay with you?"

Drake looked away fast, lips pursed in a silent whistle. Behind him he heard Beau's comment.

"Does that mean you and I are now finished?"

Mai's voice remained calm. "I guess that's up to Matt to decide."

Oh thanks. Thanks a bloody bunch.

It came almost with a tone of relief when his own phone rang. "Yes?"

"Marsh here. Are my little soldiers ready for a brisk jog?"

"You killed those innocent people. When we meet I will see you answer for that."

"No, friend, it is you who are about to answer. You read my demands, yes? Five hundred million. It is a fair sum for a city full of men, women and little tykes."

Drake closed his eyes, grating his teeth. "What next?"

"Details for the payment, naturally. Go to Grand Central Station. They're waiting inside one of the central cafés." He mentioned the name. "Folded neatly and tucked inside an envelope which some kind soul has stuck to the underside of the last table at the far end of the counter. Trust me, you'll understand when you get there."

"And if we don't?" Drake hadn't forgotten about the escaped cell member nor the existence of at least two further cells.

"Then I'll call on the next donkey to carry my load and blow up a donut shop. That sound okay with you?"

Drake fantasized for a moment about what he might do to Marsh when they captured him. "How long?"

"Oh, ten minutes should do it."

"Ten minutes? That's bollocks, Marsh, and you know it. Grand Central is over twenty minutes from here. Probably double that."

"I never said you had to walk."

Drake clenched his fists. They were being set up to fail and they all knew it.

"Tell you what," Marsh said. "To prove I can be pliable I'll change that to twelve minutes. And counting . . ."

Drake started to run.

CHAPTER NINETEEN

Drake rushed into the road as Beau called up the coordinates for Grand Central on his GPS. Alicia and Mai ran a step behind. This time however, Drake wasn't planning on making the journey on the hoof. Despite the impossibly crushing schedule Marsh had set the attempt had to be made. Three cars had been abandoned outside the museum, two Corollas and a Civic. The Yorkshireman didn't give them a second glance. What he wanted was something . . .

"Get in!" Alicia was standing by the open door of the Civic.

"Not nippy enough," he said.

"We can't waste time standing here waiting for—"

"That'll do," Drake saw beyond a slow-moving horse and carriage ride that had just exited Central Park to where a powerful F150 pickup idled away at the curb.

He sprinted toward it.

Alicia and Mai took off behind. "Is he fucking kidding?" Alicia ranted at Mai. "No way am I riding a horse. No way!"

They slipped past the animal and made short work of requesting the driver lend them his vehicle. Drake jumped on the gas pedal, burning rubber as he shot away from the curb. Beau pointed to the right.

"Take that through Central Park. It's the 79th Street

Transverse and leads to Madison Avenue."

"Love that song," Alicia barked. "And where's Tiffany's? I'm hungry."

Beau gave her an odd look. "It isn't a restaurant, Myles."

"And Madison Avenue was a pop group," Drake said. "Led by Cheyne Coates. As if anyone would ever forget her." He swallowed with a flash of memory.

Alicia grunted. "Bollocks. I'm just gonna stop trying to lighten the mood. Any why is that, Drakey? Was she a tart?"

"Hey, steady on!" He swung the speeding vehicle onto 79th, which was a single wide lane and lined by a high wall with trees overhanging. "A pinup maybe. And a remarkable front woman."

"Look out!"

Mai's warning saved their vehicle as a Silverado swerved over the inch-high central reserve and tried to ram them. Drake caught sight of the face behind the wheel—the last member of the third cell. He tramped on the gas pedal, jerking everyone back into their seats as the other vehicle spun and set off in pursuit. All of a sudden their race through Central Park took on a far deadlier aspect.

The driver of the Silverado drove with reckless abandonment. Drake slowed to ease past a scattering of cabs, but their pursuer used the opportunity to slam their rear end. The F150 jolted and swerved but then righted itself without issue. The Silverado side-swiped a cab, sending it spinning over into the other roadway where it smashed into the retaining wall.

Drake turned sharply left and then right to pass a dog-leg of cabs and then accelerated along an open stretch of road.

The terrorist behind them leaned out of his window, gun in hand.

"Down!" Drake yelled.

Bullets hammered every surface—the car, the road, the walls and the trees. The man was wild with anger and excitement and probably hatred too, uncaring as to the damage he caused. Beau, in the back seat of the F150, pulled a Glock and shot the back window out. Cold air rushed into the cab.

A row of buildings appeared to the left and then several pedestrians sauntering along the sidewalk up ahead. Drake saw only the Devil's choice now—the chance death of a passerby or be late to Grand Central and face the consequences.

Eight minutes left.

Tearing down 79th, Drake spied a short tunnel ahead, overhung by hanging green branches. As they entered the brief darkness he hit the brake pedal, hoping their pursuer would swerve into the wall or at least lose his gun in the chaos. Instead, he veered around them, driving hard, shooting out of the side window as he went past.

They all ducked as their own window blew in, the whine of a bullet almost gone before they heard it. Alicia hung her own head out now, gun aimed, and fired at the Silverado. Ahead, it sped up and then slowed. Drake closed the gap fast. Another bridge appeared and now traffic was steady on both sides of the double yellow lines. Drake closed the gap until their own fender was almost touching the rear of the other car.

The terrorist twisted his frame around and pointed the gun over his shoulder.

Alicia fired first, the bullet pulverizing the Silverado's rear window. The driver must have flinched, for his vehicle swerved, narrowly missing oncoming traffic and inspiring a tuneful burst of horns. Alicia leaned further out.

"That bit of blond hair whipping about," Mai said. "Just reminds me of something. What do they call them now? A . . . collie?"

More shots. The terrorist fired back. Drake used evasive driving techniques as safely as he could. The traffic ahead was thinning out again and he used the chance to power past the Silverado, snaking over to the wrong side of the road. At his back, Mai powered down a window and emptied a clip into the other vehicle. Drake swung back in and studied the rear view.

"He's still coming."

Unexpectedly, Central Park ended and the busy crossroads at Fifth Avenue seemed to jump out at them. Cars were slowing, stopped, and pedestrians sauntered along at the crossings and lined the sidewalks. Drake grabbed a quick glimpse of the yellow-painted stoplights currently at green.

Super-long white buses lined both sides of Fifth Avenue. Drake braked hard, but the terrorist again slammed into their taillights. Through the wheel he felt the back end twitching around, saw the potential for disaster, and wrenched against the spin to regain control. The vehicle righted as it shot through the intersection, the Silverado only an inch behind.

A bus tried to pull out in front of them, giving Drake no choice but to scrape down its entire left-hand side and chance the center of the road. Metal screeched and glass scattered across his lap. The Silverado crashed along in his wake.

"Five minutes," Beau said quietly.

With no time he piled on the speed. Soon, Madison Avenue hove into view, the gray-fronted Chase bank and black-canvased J.Crew's filling his field of vision ahead.

"Two more yet," Beau said.

Together, the racing vehicles sped from small gap to small gap, smashing vehicles aside and swerving around slower obstacles. Drake leaned constantly on the horn, wishing he had a siren of some sort and Alicia fired into the air to make pedestrians and drivers move quickly aside. NYPD cars were already screaming in their devastating wake. He'd already noticed the only vehicles that seemed to be treated with respect were the big red fire trucks.

"Up ahead," Beau said.

"Got it," Drake saw a gap opening up onto Lexington Avenue and went for it. Gunning the engine he drifted the vehicle hard around the corner. Smoke flew from the tires, making people scream all along the sidewalk. Here, on the new road, vehicles were parked end to end on both sides and a chaos of flatbeds, vans and one-way streets kept even the best drivers guessing.

"Not far now," Beau said.

Drake saw his chance ahead as the traffic thinned. "Mai," he said. "Do you remember Bangkok?"

As seamless as a supercar gear-change, Mai slammed a new mag into her Glock and unfastened her seatbelt, shuffling around in her seat. Alicia stared at Drake and Drake stared into the rearview. The Silverado was coming hard, trying to ram them as they approached Grand Central and a swarming crowd.

Mai rose in her seat, angling her body out of the already smashed rear window and starting to push.

Alicia nudged Drake. "Bangkok?"

"It's not what you think."

"Oh, it never is. You'll be telling me what happened in Thailand stays in Thailand next."

Mai slithered through the small gap, ripping her clothes but forcing her body on. Drake saw the moment when the wind hit her, when the grit stung her eyes. He saw the moment when the chasing terrorist blinked in shock.

The Silverado came on, shockingly close.

Mai jumped down to the bed of the truck, legs apart, and raised her weapon. She took a sighting and then started firing from the back of the truck, bullets smashing through the other car's windows. Buildings and buses and lampposts passed leisurely by. Mai pulled her trigger again and again, ignoring the wind and the car's motion, focusing only on the man who would otherwise kill them.

Drake kept the wheel as steady as possible, the speed constant. For once no cars rolled before them, something he'd prayed for. Mai's feet were planted and her concentration necessarily absorbed by one thing only. Drake was her guide.

"Now!" he shouted at the top of his voice.

Alicia twisted around like a child who'd lost a candy down the seatback. "What's she gonna do?"

Drake applied the brakes very softly, a millimeter at a time. Mai rammed in a second mag and then started running up the bed of the truck, straight for the tailgate. The Silverado's driver's eyes widened even further as he saw the wild ninja running straight at his speeding vehicle from another!

Mai reached the tailgate and leapt into the air, legs pumping, arms windmilling. There was a moment before gravity tugged her down when she arced gracefully though thin air, a vision of stealth and skill and beauty, but then she came down hard onto the hood of the other man's car. Instantly, she buckled, allowing her legs and knees to take the impact and help steady her. Ungiving metal was a tough place to land, and Mai fell forward fast toward the jagged windshield.

The Silverado driver was braking hard, but still managed to bring his gun toward her face.

Mai spread her knees as the sudden impact passed through her, strengthening her spine and shoulders. Her weapon remained in her hands, already pointing at the terrorist. Two shots and he grunted, his foot still on the brake pedal, blood soaking through the front of his shirt and slumping forward.

Mai crawled up the hood of the car, reached inside the windshield and dragged the driver through. No way was she allowing him the courtesy of recuperation. His pain-filled eyes met hers and tried to lock on.

"How . . . how did you—"

Mai punched him in the face. Then she held on as the car coasted into the back of Drake's. The Englishman had deliberately slowed in order to 'catch' the driverless car before it slewed in some dangerous, random direction.

"So that's what you did in Bangkok?" Alicia asked.

"Something like that."

"And what happened next?"

Drake looked away. "Not a clue, love."

They flung open the doors, double-parking alongside a cab, as close to Grand Central as they could possibly get. Civilians backed away, gawping at them. The sensible ones turned to run. Dozens more took out cellphones and started to take pictures. Drake jumped to the sidewalk and broke instantly into a sprint.

"Time's up," Beauregard muttered at his side.

CHAPTER TWENTY

Drake charged though into the main hall of Grand Central station. The vast space yawned to left and right and high above. Shiny surfaces and polished floors were a shock to the system, departure and arrivals boards flickered all around and the rush of humanity seemed incessant. Beau reminded them of the name of the café and showed them a floor plan of the terminal.

"Main concourse," Mai said. "Turn right, past the escalators."

Rushing, twisting, performing amazing acrobatic feats just to avoid a collision, the team tore through the station. Minutes passed. Coffee shops, Belgian chocolate stores and bagel stalls whipped by, their combined aromas making Drake's head spin. They entered what was known as Lexington Passage and started to slow.

"There!"

Alicia sprinted now, squeezing through a narrow entry into one of the smallest cafés Drake had ever seen. Almost unconsciously his mind ticked off the tables. Not hard, there were only three.

Alicia pushed a man wearing a gray overcoat aside, then fell to her knees beside the black surface. The top was littered with a discarded clutter, the chairs set back slapdash style. Alicia felt around underneath and soon came up holding a white envelope, her gaze hopeful.

Drake had been watching from several spaces away, but not the Englishwoman. Instead, he had been surveying the staff and the customers, those who passed outside—and one other place in particular.

The door to the back office.

It opened now, an inquisitive female figure poking her head out. Almost immediately she locked eyes with the only man staring right at her—Matt Drake.

No . . .

She held up a portable phone. *I think this is for you*, she mouthed.

Drake nodded, still watching the entire area. Alicia ripped open the envelope and then frowned.

"This can't be right."

Mai stared. "What? Why not?"

"It says—boom!"

CHAPTER TWENTY ONE

Drake raced to the phone and snatched it away from the woman. "What are you playing at?"

Marsh giggled down the line. "Have you checked under the other two tables?"

Then the line went dead. Drake felt everything inside him collapse as his soul and his heart froze, but he didn't stop moving. "The tables!" he cried out and broke into a sprint, dropping and sliding on his knees under the closest one.

Alicia screamed at the staff and the patrons to get out, to evacuate. Beau collapsed under the other table. Drake no doubt saw an exact copy of what the Frenchman locked eyes upon, a small explosive device stuck to the underside of the table with duct tape. About the size and shape of a water bottle, it was crudely covered in old Christmas wrapping paper. The message *Ho Ho Ho!* was not lost on Drake.

Alicia fell in beside him. "How do we defuse the sucker? And more importantly, *can* we defuse the sucker?"

"You know what I know, Myles. In the Army we usually blew one bomb up with another. It's the safest way, mostly. But this guy knew what he was doing. Wrapped well in an innocuous package. See the wires? They're all the same color. Blasting cap. Remote detonator. Not sophisticated but dammed dangerous."

"So grow a set and stop the bloody blasting cap from going off."

"Grow a set? Shit, we're totally winging it here." Drake looked up, and saw with unbelieving eyes a crowd of people with their faces pressed to the café windows. Some were even trying to get through the open door. The customary android phones were recording what might be their owners' own deaths in only a few minutes time.

"Get out!" he shouted, and Alicia joined him. "Evacuate this building now!"

At last, scared faces turned away and started to get the message. Drake remembered the size and scale of the main hall and the mass of people inside and gritted his teeth until the roots hurt.

"How long do you think?" Alicia hunkered down beside him again.

"Minutes, if that."

Drake stared at the device. Truth be told it didn't look sophisticated, just a simple bomb designed to scare rather than maim. He'd seen firework bombs of this size and probably with the same rudimentary detonation device. His army experience might be a little rusty, but faced with a red-wire-blue-wire situation it soon came flooding back.

Except all the wires are the same color.

Mayhem washed all around his self-imposed cocoon. Like a tell-tale whisper, word of a bomb swept through the great halls, and one man's flight to freedom infected the next and the next until all except the hardiest—or stupidest—of commuters were heading for the exit. The noise was tremendous, washing up to the high rafters and right back down the walls. Men and women fell in the rush and were helped up by passersby. Some panicked and others stayed calm. Bosses tried to keep their staff in place but were justifiably fighting a losing battle. Crowds streamed out of the exits and began to fill up 42nd Street.

Drake hesitated, sweat beginning to pool along his brow. One wrong move here might lead to the loss of a limb, or more. And worse, it would put him out of the battle to take Marsh down. If the Pythian succeeded in thinning them out then he had a far better chance of achieving his ultimate goal—whatever the twisted hell that might be.

Then Beauregard squatted at his side. "Are you okay?"

Drake stared. "What the hell . . . I mean, aren't you sorting out the other—"

Beau held out the other device he'd already disarmed. "It is a simple mechanism and took but a few seconds. Would you like some help?"

Drake stared at the inner workings dangling before him, the slight smugness of the Frenchman's face, and said, "Shit. Nobody better tell the Swede this happened."

Then he pulled out the blasting cap.

Everything remained the same. A sense of relief flooded through him and he took a moment to pause and breathe. Another crisis diverted, one more small victory for the good guys. Then Alicia, her eyes on the café's counter, spoke five very distinct words.

"The fucking phone's ringing again."

And all around Grand Central, all around New York, in trash cans and under trees—even strapped to railings and finally thrown by motorcyclists—the bombs began to explode.

CHAPTER TWENTY TWO

Hayden stood before a bank of TV monitors, Kinimaka at her side. Their thoughts about breaking Ramses had temporarily been put on hold by the chase across Central Park and then the madness at Grand Central. As they watched, Moore approached them and began to comment on each monitor, the camera views labelled and able to zoom in to pick out a human hair on a freckled arm. The coverage wasn't as blanket as it should have been, but improved as Drake and his team approached the famous train station. Another monitor showed Ramses and Price in their cells, the first pacing impatiently as if he had places to be, the second sitting despondently as if all he really wanted was the offer of a noose.

Moore's team worked hard around them, calling in sightings, hunches and asking cops and agents on the street to attend certain areas. Attacks were foiled even as Hayden watched, even as Drake and Beau defused the Grand Central bombs. Moore's only way of making absolutely sure that midtown was being taken care of was to practically empty out the entire precinct.

"I don't care if it's a deaf old granny who's just lost her cat," he said. "At the very least reassure them."

"How could the cells get bombs through the metal detectors at Grand Central?" Kinimaka asked.

"Plastic explosive?" Moore ventured.

"Don't you have other measures in place for that?" Hayden asked.

"Of course, but look around you. Ninety percent of our people are looking for the goddamn nuke. I've never seen this precinct so empty."

Hayden wondered how long Marsh had been planning this. And Ramses? The terrorist prince had about five cells in New York, perhaps more, and some of those were sleeper cells. Explosives of any kind could be smuggled in at any time and just buried, concealed in the woods or in a basement for years if necessary. Look at the Russians and the verified story of their missing suitcase nukes—it was an American who hypothesized the number missing was the exact amount required to annihilate the United States. It was a Russian defector who verified they were already in America.

She took a step back, trying to encompass the whole picture. Hayden had been a law enforcement figure for most of her adult life; she felt she had witnessed every situation imaginable. But now . . . this was unprecedented. Drake had already raced from Times Square to Grand Central, saving lives by the minute and then losing two. Dahl was taking apart Ramses' cells at every turn. But it was the utter, terrifying scope of this thing that astounded her.

And the world was getting worse. She knew people who didn't bother watching the news anymore, people who had deleted the apps from their phones, because everything they saw was sickening and they felt there was nothing they could do. Decisions that were clear and obvious from the beginning, particularly with the emergence of IS, never happened, clouded by politics, gain and greed, and discounting the depth of human suffering. What the public now wanted was honesty, a figure they could trust, someone who came with as much transparency as was safely manageable.

Hayden took it all in. Her feeling of helplessness was akin to the emotions she'd been subjected to by Tyler Webb of late. The sense of being so cleverly stalked and powerless to do anything about it. She experienced the same emotions now as she watched Drake and Dahl try to bring New York and the rest of the world back from the edge.

"I will kill Ramses for this," she said.

Kinimaka laid an enormous paw on her shoulders. "Let me. I'm much less pretty than you and would fare better in prison."

Moore gestured at a particular screen. "Look there, guys. They've disarmed the bomb."

Elation shot through Hayden as she watched Matt Drake emerge from the café with a relieved and victorious look on his face. The assembled team cheered and then suddenly paused as events began to spiral out of control.

On many monitors, Hayden saw bins exploding, cars swerving to avoid erupting manhole covers. She saw motorcyclists veering through traffic and throwing brick shaped objects at buildings and windows. Seconds later another explosion occurred. She saw a car raise several feet off the floor as a bomb detonated underneath, smoke and flames billowing out from the sides. All around Grand Central, amid the fleeing commuters, trashcans burst into flame. The purpose was terror, not casualties. Fires burned on two bridges, causing tailbacks so profuse even motorcycles couldn't thread a path through.

Moore stared, face slackening for just a second before he began to bark out orders. Hayden fought to keep her tough perspective and felt Mano's shoulder brushing against her own.

We will go on.

Activity continued in the ops center, emergency services dispatched and law enforcement rerouted to the worst hit areas. The Fire Department and Bomb Squad were stretched beyond all limits. Moore ordered the use of choppers to help patrol the streets. When the Macy's department store was hit by another small device Hayden could watch no more.

She turned away, searching through all her experience for any kind of clue as to what to do next, remembering Hawaii and Washington DC in recent years, focusing . . . but then a terrible sound, a horrendous drawn-out noise, drew her attention back to the screens.

"No!"

CHAPTER TWENTY THREE

Hayden barged through the people around her and burst out of the room. Almost growling with anger she descended the stairs, fists compressed into hard lumps of flesh and bone. Kinimaka shouted a warning but Hayden ignored it. She would do this and the world would be a better, safer place.

Surging down the corridor that stretched under the precinct she finally came to Ramses' cell. The bastard was still laughing, the noise nothing short of a monster's terrible snarl. Somehow he knew what was happening. The pre-planning was obvious, but the utter contempt for human welfare was not something she could deal with lightly.

Hayden flung open the door to his room. The guard jumped and then shot outside in response to her order. Hayden stalked right up to the iron bars.

"Tell me what is happening. Tell me now and I'll go easy on you."

Ramses guffawed. "What is happening?" He faked an American accent. "Is that you people are being brought to your knees. And you will stay there," The large man bent low so that he could stare right into Hayden's eyes from a few millimeters distant. "With your tongue hanging out. Doing everything I tell you to do."

Hayden unlocked the cell door. Ramses didn't

waste a moment, rushing her and trying to knock her to the floor. The man's hands were cuffed but that didn't stop him from using his enormous bulk. Hayden sidestepped smartly and rolled him into one of the vertical iron bars, head first, the impact snapping his neck backward. Then she punched hard to the kidneys and the spine, making him flinch and groan.

No more insane laughter.

Hayden used him as a punch bag, moving around his frame and battering different areas. When Ramses roared and spun, she made the first three punches count—bleeding nose, bruised jaw and throat. Ramses began to choke. Hayden didn't let up, even as Kinimaka reached her side and urged a little caution.

"Stop fucking bleating, Mano," Hayden snapped at him. "There're people dying out there."

Ramses tried to laugh, but the pain in his larynx stopped him. Hayden added to it with a swift rabbit punch. "Laugh now."

Kinimaka dragged her away. Hayden turned on him, but then the seemingly damaged Ramses charged them both. He was a big man, even taller than Kinimaka, their muscle mass evenly matched, but the Hawaiian outmatched the terrorist in one crucial area.

Battle experience.

Ramses collided with Kinimaka and then rebounded badly, staggering away and back into his cell. "What the hell are you made of?" he muttered.

"Harder stuff than you," Kinimaka said, rubbing the impact area.

"We want to know what's next," Hayden pressed, following Ramses back into his cell. "We want to know about the nuke. Where is it? Who has control? What are their orders? And for God's sake, what are your true intentions?"

Ramses fought hard to remain upright, clearly not wanting to fall to his knees. The strain stood out in every sinew. When he did raise himself up though, his head hung. Hayden remained as wary as she would be of an injured snake.

"There is nothing you can do. Ask your man, Price. He already knows this. He knows everything. New York will burn, lady, and my people will dance our victory jig amidst the smoldering ashes."

Price? Hayden saw treachery at every turn. Someone was lying and that made her anger seethe even more. Not falling for the poison that dripped from this man's lips she held a hand out to Mano.

"Go get me a Taser."

"Hayden—"

"Just do it!" She turned, fury radiating from every pore. "Fetch me a Taser and man the fuck up."

In her past, Hayden destroyed those relationships where she considered her partner too weak. Most notably the one she shared with Ben Blake, who died at the hands of the Blood King's men only months later. Ben, she had thought, was too young, inexperienced, somewhat immature, but even with Kinimaka she now started to adjust her perspective. She saw him as weak, lacking and certainly in need of readjustment.

"Do not fight me, Mano. Just do it."

A whisper but it reached the Hawaiian's ears just fine. The big man trotted off, hiding his face and his emotions from her. Hayden swung her gaze back to Ramses.

"You are like me now," he said. "I have made one more disciple."

"Ya think?" Hayden buried her knee into the other's abdomen, her elbow then slamming down without mercy into the back of his neck. "Would a disciple beat the crap out of you?"

"If my hands were free . . ."

"Really?" Hayden was blind with rage. "Let's see what you can do shall we?"

As she reached around for Ramses' cuffs, Kinimaka returned, a Taser looking like a cigar in his clasped fist. He saw her intentions and stood back.

"What?" she cried.

"You do what you have to do."

Hayden cursed the man, and then cursed even more loudly into Ramses' face, the feeling of frustration high at not being able to break him.

A low, calm voice broke through her rage: *Still, maybe he did give you a clue.*

Maybe.

Hayden pushed Ramses until he fell onto his bunk, a new idea springing to mind. Yes, there might be a way. Glaring at Kinimaka she exited the cell, locked it, and then walked toward the outer door.

"Anything new happening up top?"

"More trashcan bombs, but fewer now. One more

motorcyclist but they grabbed him."

Hayden's thought process grew clearer. She stepped out into the corridor and then approached the other door. Without stopping she pushed through, confident Robert Price would have heard the commotion coming from Ramses' cell. The look in his eyes told her that he had.

"I don't know anything," he blustered. "Please, believe me. If he told you I knew something, anything, about the nuke then he is lying."

Hayden reached for the Taser. "Who to believe? The terrorist madman or the treasonous politician. Actually, let's see what the Taser tells us."

"No!" Price threw up both hands.

Hayden aimed. "You may not know what's happening in New York, Robert, so I'll lay it all out for you. Just once. Terror cells are in control of a nuclear weapon which we believe they have the capability to detonate at any moment. Now, also, a bonkers Pythian thinks he is actually in control. Small explosions are occurring across Manhattan. Bombs were planted at Grand Central. And, Robert, it isn't over yet."

The ex-Secretary gawped, quite unable to form words. In her newfound clarity Hayden was almost convinced he was telling the truth. But that one shred of doubt remained, nagging at her repeatedly like a small child.

The man was a successful politician.

She fired the Taser. It shot off and away, missing the man by an inch. Price shook in his boots.

"The next one will go below the belt," Hayden promised.

Then, as Price teared up, as Mano grunted and she remembered Ramses' demonic laughter, as she thought about all the terror coursing through Manhattan right now and her colleagues out there in the thick of it, at the very heart of jeopardy, it was Hayden Jaye who broke.

No more. I will not take this for one more minute.

Grabbing Price, she threw him against a wall, the force of the impact sending him to his knees. Kinimaka hauled him up, throwing her a questioning glance.

"Just get out of my way."

Again, she threw Price, this time at the outer door. He bounced off, whimpering, falling, and then she had hold of him again, steering him out into the corridor and towards Ramses' cell. When Price saw the terrorist locked in his cell he started to whine, to grovel. Hayden forced him forward.

"Please, please you can't do this."

"Actually," Kinimaka said. "This is something we can do."

"Nooo!"

Hayden threw Price against the bars and unlocked the cell. Ramses didn't move, still seated on his bunk and reviewing proceedings under hooded eyes. Kinimaka took out his Glock and covered both men as Hayden unlocked their bonds.

"One chance," she said. "One prison cell. Two men. The first to call me for a chat gets it easy. Do you understand?"

Price bleated like a poorly calf. Ramses still hadn't moved. To Hayden the sight of him was unnerving. The sudden change in him was ludicrous. She walked away and locked the cell, leaving both men together as her phone squawked and Agent Moore's voice came over the line.

"Come up here, Jaye. You have to see this."

"What is it?" She ran with Kinimaka, chasing their shadows out of the cellblocks and back up the stairs.

"More bombs," he said despondently. "I've sent everyone to deal with the mess. And this latest demand ain't what we expected it to be. Oh, and your man Dahl has a lead on the fourth cell. He's chasing it down right now."

"On our way!" Hayden sped toward the precinct floor.

CHAPTER TWENTY FOUR

Dahl threw himself into the passenger seat and let Smyth drive; Kenzie, Lauren and Yorgi again in back. Even as they threaded their way back towards the precinct, reports of Drake hitting Grand Central were coming in, but he heard nothing beyond that. Moore had just called in one more tip from an informant—the fourth terrorist cell was operating out of an upscale apartment building near Central Park, and now that Dahl thought about it, it stood to reason that some of these cells would be funded differently to others—it helped them blend in—but Dahl wondered how a bunch of people could exist inside a specific society so easily without remembering their brainwashing indoctrinations. Brainwashing was a particular art and he doubted your typical terrorist had mastered it just yet.

Don't be so naive.

Moore's infiltrators were risking more than just exposure to get these tips out. The repercussions of this day would reverberate indefinitely, and he hoped Homeland had a handle on where it would all wash out. If an undercover got himself burned today his problems were just beginning.

Traffic cops, always prevalent around intersections, were trying their best to filter the traffic, facing enormous and probably insurmountable problems, but aware emergency vehicles had to be given priority. Dahl saw several little viewing platforms – almost like mini cherry pickers – where cops directed their colleagues from their higher vantage point, and he nodded his thanks as they were waved through.

Dahl checked the car's GPS. "Eight minutes," he said. "We ready?"

"Ready," the whole team returned.

"Lauren, Yorgi stay with the car this time. We can't risk you anymore."

"I'm coming," Lauren said. "You need the backup."

Dahl forced down images of the basement and the SWAT leader's death. "We can't risk unnecessary lives. Lauren, Yorgi you have your value in different areas. Just watch the exterior. We need eyes there too."

"You might need my skills," Yorgi said.

"I doubt we'll be hopping across balconies, Yorgi. Or using drainpipes. Just . . ." He sighed. "Please do as I ask and watch the bloody exterior. Don't force me to make it an order."

An uneasy silence fell. Each team member processed the events from the previous assault entirely differently, but since it had all happened only a half hour ago most were still in the shock stage. The observations were endless—how close they had come to being blown up. How a man had so selflessly sacrificed himself to save their lives. How cheaply these terrorists regarded all forms of life.

Dahl found his mind returning to that old saw—how could an adult imbue such hateful traits into the youngest child? The most innocent mind? How could a grown up, responsible person believe it was right to warp such fragile minds, alter the course of a promising life forever? To replace it with . . . what? . . . hatred, inflexibility, fanaticism.

However we look at it, whatever our views on religion, Dahl thought, *the Devil truly does walk among us.*

Smyth hauled on the brakes as they approached a high-rise. Prepping and exiting the car took seconds, and left all of them exposed on the sidewalk. Dahl felt uneasy, knowing the fourth cell were almost certainly inside and how competent they appeared to be. His eyes fell upon Lauren and Yorgi.

"What the hell are you doing? Get back in the car."

They drew near the doorman, showed their IDs and asked about two apartments on the fourth floor. Both belonged to a young couple who kept themselves to themselves and were always polite. The doorman had never even seen both couples together, but yes one of the apartments did receive regular visitors. He thought it was some kind of social night, but then he wasn't exactly paid to be over inquisitive.

Dahl moved him gently aside and headed for the stairs. The doorman asked if they needed a key.

Dahl smiled softly. "That won't be necessary."

Four floors were dealt with easily and then the three soldiers paced carefully down the corridor. It was as Dahl saw the correct apartment number come into view that his cell started to vibrate.

"What?" Smyth and Kenzie waited, covering their periphery.

Moore's tired voice filled Dahl's head. "The tip is

false. Some informant fingering the wrong people for a bit of revenge. Sorry, I just found out."

"False," Dahl breathed. "Are you kidding me? We're stood outside their fucking door with HKs."

"Then leave. The informant loves one of the women. Whatever, just get back on the road, Dahl. This next tip's red hot."

The Swede cursed and pulled his team back, concealed their weapons and then hurried past the surprised doorman. Dahl had actually considered asking the doorman to conduct a quiet evacuation before they ascended to the fourth floor—knowing what might happen up there—and now wondered how the residents might have reacted to find out his tip was fraudulent.

An interesting social question. What type of person would complain at being thrown out of their homes whilst police searched for terrorists . . . if that search proved ultimately based on a lie?

Dahl shrugged it off. Moore wasn't exactly on his shit list yet, but the man was teetering on stony ground. "This next lead's going to pan out, yes?" He spoke into the still-open line.

"It should. Same guy who fingered the third cell. Just get to Times Square and fast."

"There's a threat against Times Square? Which security forces are in place already?"

"All of them."

"All right, we're ten minutes out."

"Make it five."

Smyth drove like a demon, cutting corners and

squeezing, even scraping, between badly parked cars. They abandoned the vehicle at 50th and ran, now against the crowd as it swept away from Times Square, the cheerful façades of M&M's World, Hershey's Chocolate World and even a street-corner Starbucks now undermined by the overhanging threat. Enormous billboards shone thousands of multi-colored images back and forth above head-height across the street, each vying for attention and engaged in a lively, vibrant battle. The team threaded a forest of scaffold poles as almost every other shop seemed to be undergoing some kind of renovation. Dahl tried to figure out a way to keep Lauren and Yorgi safe, but the drive and the run made it nigh on impossible. Like it or not, they were all soldiers now, the team strengthened by their presence.

Ahead cops were stringing a cordon around the square. New Yorkers looked on with bewilderment and visitors were told to return to their hotels.

"It's just a precaution, ma'am," Dahl heard one of the uniforms saying.

And then the world went to hell again. Four tourists, perusing the windows around Levis and Bubba Gump, dropped their backpacks, rooted around inside and came up with automatic weapons. Dahl ducked behind a street kiosk as he unstrapped his own weapon.

Gunfire echoed around Times Square. Windows smashed and billboards were peppered, destroyed because the majority were screens now, the largest in the world, and the epitome of capitalism. Mortar rained down upon the sidewalk. Those who remained and the security services scrambled for cover. Dahl poked his head out and returned a salvo, his shots untargeted but causing the terrorists to curse loudly and look for cover of their own.

On to you straight away this time, Dahl thought with grim satisfaction. *No hope for you.*

Dahl saw the cell duck behind a parked cab and noted the bus abandoned alongside. He had never visited Times Square before, and only seen it briefly on the TV, but to see such a clearly pedestrian-friendly area so empty was unnerving. More shots rang out as cell members no doubt saw people moving inside the shops and office buildings. Dahl moved quietly into the street.

Beyond the bus and alongside the far sidewalk other security forces were getting into place. More SWAT, black-suited agents and NYPD cops were maneuvering around to some quiet, choreographed beat. Dahl signaled them to get into line. What passed for signage here clearly didn't translate because nobody took a moment's notice of the mad Swede.

"We waiting for those three-and-four-letter pussies, or are we gonna make these fuckers burn?" Kenzie grated at his side.

Dahl turned away from the American agents. "I do enjoy your bright terminology," he said, creeping in the shadow of the bus. "But sparingly."

"So you want to keep me around now. I get it."

"I didn't say that."

Smyth lay flat on the ground peering under vehicles. "I see legs."

"Can you be sure they're terrorist legs?" Dahl asked.

"I think so but, hell, it's not as if they're labelled."

"They will be soon," Kenzie hefted her rifle as if it were the sword she so craved and paused behind one of the bus's giant wheels. The team took one communal breath.

Dahl peeked out. "I do believe it's that time again."

Kenzie went first, racing around the back of the bus and charging the yellow cab. Automatic gunfire rang out, but it was directed at windows and bus stops and anywhere else the terrorists figured defenseless people might be taking cover. Dahl thanked their lucky stars that no lookout had been posted, knowing speed was their ally here in taking down the cell, which had to be done before they switched to grenades or worse. Kenzie and he rounded the cab, eyeballing the four men who reacted surprisingly quickly. Instead of swinging their weapons around they just charged, slamming into Dahl and Kenzie and knocking them off their feet. Bodies sprawled across the road. Dahl caught a descending fist and deflected it away, hearing the knuckles impact hard against tarmac. Still, the second arm came down, this one with the rifle butt upended. Dahl couldn't trap this one, nor glance it away, so reverted to the only action open to him.

He lowered his forehead and took the blow upon his skull.

Blackness writhed before his eyes, pain ricocheted from nerve to nerve, but the Swede didn't allow any of that to interfere with his job. The weapon struck and then came away, vulnerable. Dahl grabbed it and wrenched against the man who held it. Blood trickled down both sides of his face. The man brought a fist down again, this time a bit more timidly, and Dahl caught it in his own fist and began to squeeze.

With every fiber in his being, every sinew of every knuckle stretched taut.

Bones broke like twigs snapping. The terrorist screamed and tried to pull his hand away but Dahl would have none of it. They needed this cell taken out of commission. Fast. Gripping down even harder he made sure the man's attention was completely encompassed by the overpowering pain in his fist and yanked free his Glock.

One down.

The gun discharged three bullets before the terrorist's eyes glazed over. Dahl heaved him away and then rose up like the avenging angel, blood spilling from his skull and a snarl of intent warping his features.

Kenzie fought a large man, their guns trapped between their bodies, and faces almost mashed together. Smyth pounded on the third, driving the guy to his knees as he struck with almost perfect, precise fury. The final terrorist had gotten the better of Lauren, throwing her to the ground, and was trying to line up a shot when Yorgi flung himself in front of the barrel.

Dahl caught his breath.

The gun went off. Yorgi collapsed, struck in the vest. Dahl then saw that the situation was slightly different to how he had first read it. Yorgi hadn't jumped athletically in front of a bullet, he had rammed the terrorist's shooting arm with his whole body.

Different, but still effective.

Dahl leapt to the Russian's aid, striking the gunman under the left arm and taking his feet off the ground. The Swede built up momentum and speed, bunching his muscles, carrying his load with a ferocity born of displeasure. Three feet and then six and the terrorist was being propelled fast when he finally impacted head-first with the menu board of the Hard Rock Café. The plastic split, drenched with blood, as Dahl's crazy momentum cracked his opponent's skull and tore at flesh. Kinimaka might not have liked it, but the Swede had used an American icon to neutralize a terrorist.

Karma.

Dahl whirled again, now dripping blood from his ears and chin. Kenzie and her opponent were still locked in mortal contest, but Smyth's had managed to open a gap between the soldier and himself by rolling several times. On the final revolution he fought to wrestle his weapon around, got lucky, and ended up with the pointy end aimed straight at Smyth.

Dahl roared, bounding in, but there was nothing he could do about the shot. In the blink of an eye the terrorist fired and the onrushing Smyth took a bullet that stopped him dead, sending him to his knees.

Bringing his forehead in line for the next shot.

The terrorist squeezed the trigger, but at that instant Dahl arrived—a seething, mobile mountain—and smashed the terrorist between himself and a wall.

Bones broke and grated together, blood gouted, and the rifle clattered away. When Dahl started, stricken, toward Smyth he saw and heard the angry soldier swearing loudly.

He's okay then.

Saved by the Kevlar vest, Smyth had still taken a short-range bullet and would have a bruise almost to die for, but their new avant-garde body armor had taken the sting out of it. Dahl wiped his face, now registering the approach of a SWAT team.

Kenzie wrestled her opponent this way and that, the larger man struggling to match her for dexterity and downright brawn. Dahl stood back with a faint smile on his face.

One of the SWAT guys ran up. "Does she need help?"

"Nah, she's just fooling around. Leave her be."

Kenzie caught the exchange from the corner of her eye and gnashed her already gritted teeth. It was plain the two were evenly matched but the Swede was testing her, gauging her commitment to the team and even herself. Was she worthy?

She wrenched at the gun and then let go as her opponent wrenched back, making him overbalance, bringing a knee up into his ribs and an elbow to his nose. Her next blow was a chop to the wrist and then a lightning fast grab. As the man struggled and groaned she bent the wrist back hard, heard the snap and saw the gun fall to the floor. Still he fought, withdrawing a knife and thrusting at her chest. Kenzie squeezed it all in, felt the blade nick the flesh over her ribs, and spun around, taking him with her. The knife pulled back for a second thrust but this time she was ready. She took hold of the extracted arm, spun under it and wrenched it around behind the man's back. Without mercy she pushed until it also broke and left the terrorist helpless. Swiftly, she plucked two grenades from his belt and then stuffed one down the front of his trousers and into his boxer shorts.

Dahl, watching, found a scream tearing into his throat. "Noooo!"

Kenzie's fingers came out with the firing pin.

"We don't do that, you—"

"Now watcha gonna do," Kenzie whispered up close, "with your arms all broken and stuff? Ain't gonna hurt anyone now are ya, asshole?"

Dahl didn't know whether to stick or twist, bolt, or dive headlong, grab Kenzie or leap for cover. In the end the seconds ticked by and nothing exploded except Smyth's particularly short fuse.

"Are you kidding me?" he bellowed. "What the fu—"

"Fake," Kenzie flicked the firing pin at Dahl's bleeding head. "Thought those perfect eagle's eyes would've spotted a dud."

"I didn't." The Swede breathed a deep sigh of relief. "Shit, Kenz, you are one fucking world-class female lunatic."

"Just give me back my katana. That always calms me down."

"Oh, yeah. I bet,"

"And this coming from you—the Mad Swede."

Dahl inclined his head. *Touché. But crap, I think I've met my match.*

By now the SWAT teams and assembled agents

were among them, and securing areas around Times Square. The team regrouped and took a few moments to catch their breath.

"Four cells down," Lauren said. "Only one to go."

"We think," Dahl said. "Best not get ahead of ourselves. And remember this final cell is the one keeping Marsh safe and probably in control of the . . ." He didn't say the word "nuke" out loud. Not here. This was the heart of Manhattan. Who knew what parabolic mics might be scattered around?

"Good job, guys," he said simply. "This day of hell is almost over."

But, in truth, it had barely begun.

CHAPTER TWENTY FIVE

Julian Marsh figured that, without a doubt, he was the happiest man alive. Directly in front of him lay a primed, trussed up nuclear weapon, close enough to touch, his to play with on a whim. To his left curled a divine, beautiful woman, also his to play with on a whim. And she to play with him of course, though a particular area was starting to get a little sore from all the attention. Maybe some of that whipped cream . . .

But continuing on his previous and most important train of thought—a passive terrorist cell sat near the window, again his to play with on a whim. And then there was the American government, chasing their tails all over the city, running scared and running blind, his to play—

"Julian?" Zoe breathed a hair's breadth from his left ear. "Want me to head down south again?"

"Sure, but don't inhale the bastard like you did last time. Give him a little breathing space, eh?"

"Ooh, of course."

Marsh let her have her fun, and then thought about what would happen next. Mid-morning had already passed, and certain deadlines were approaching. The time was almost here when he would unwrap another burner cell and call Homeland with the dead-drop demands. Of course, he knew there would be no actual "dead-drop", not with five hundred million being exchanged, but the principal was the same and could be executed similarly. Marsh gave gratitude to the gods of sin and iniquity. With those guys on your side what couldn't be accomplished?

Like all good dreams this one would come to an end, but Marsh determined that he would enjoy it while it lasted.

Patting Zoe on the head and then standing up, he untied one of his shoe laces and walked over to the window. With two minds often came two different viewpoints, but both of Marsh's personalities were au fait with this scenario. How could either of them lose? He'd pilfered one of Zoe's condoms and now tried to pull it over one hand. In the end he gave in and made do with two fingers. Hell, it still satisfied his inner quirkiness.

As he wondered what to do with the spare shoelace, the cell leader rose and stared over at him, giving Marsh a blank smile. This was Gator, or as Marsh privately referred to him—the Gatorous One—and, though quiet and clearly slow, he did have a look of danger about him. Marsh guessed he was probably one of the vest-wearing types. A pawn. As expendable as a long piss. Marsh guffawed aloud, breaking eye contact with the Gatorous One at just the right moment.

Zoe followed in his footsteps, taking a look out the window.

"Nothing to see," Marsh said. "Lest you enjoy scrutinizing humanity's lice."

"Oh, at times they can be amusing."

Marsh looked around for his hat, the one he liked to wear canted at an angle. Of course, it had disappeared, maybe even before he reached New York. The last week had become a complete blur to him. Gator walked over and asked politely if there was anything he required.

"At the moment, no. But I will be calling them soon with details for the money transfer."

"You will?"

"Yes. Didn't I provide you people with an itinerary?" The question was rhetorical.

"Oh, that piece of crap. I have been using it as a fly swatter."

Marsh might be eccentric, crazy and driven by blood-lust, but a shallower part of him was also clever, calculating and entirely switched on. This was how he survived so well, how he made it through the Mexican tunnels. In a moment he realized he'd gauged Gator and the situation all wrong. He wasn't in charge here—they were.

And it was a moment too late.

Marsh struck out at Gator, knowing exactly where he'd left a gun, a knife and an unused Taser. Expecting success he was surprised when Gator blocked the blows and returned one of his own. Marsh took it well, ignoring the pain, and tried again. He was aware of Zoe gawping at his side and wondered why the idle bitch didn't jump in to help.

Gator again turned his punch with ease. Marsh then heard a noise at his back—the sound of the apartment door being opened. He jumped away, surprised when Gator let him, and turned.

A gasp of shock escaped his throat.

Eight men entered the apartment, all dressed in black, all carrying bags, and looking mean as foxes in a chicken run. Marsh stared and then turned to Gator, his eyes even now not quite believing what they were seeing.

"What is going on?"

"What? Did you think we would all sit nicely whilst the rich men in their tailored suits funded their wars? Well, I have news for you, big man. We do not wait for you anymore. We fund our own."

Marsh was staggered by a double blow to the face. Falling backwards, he caught hold of Zoe, expecting her to hold him up, and when she didn't they both fell to the floor. The shock of it all sent his system into overdrive, sweat glands and nerve endings in full flow and an annoying tic starting up at the corner of one eye. Took him right back to the bad old days, when he was a boy and nobody cared about him.

Gator stalked about the apartment, organizing the now twelve-strong cell. Zoe had made herself as small as possible, practically a part of the furniture as guns were revealed and other weapons of war—grenades, more than one RPG, the ever-dependable Kalashnikov, tear gas, stun-bombs and a plethora of hand-driven, steel-shod missiles. This was somewhat unnerving.

Marsh cleared his throat, still clinging to that last shred of dignity and egotism that ensured him that he, in this room, was the Satanic goat with the biggest horns.

"Look," he said. "Get your filthy hands off my nuke. Do you even know what this is, boy? Gator. Gator! We have a deadline to keep."

The leader of the fifth cell finally threw a laptop aside and strode over to Marsh. Now with backup and with the gloves well and truly off, Gator was a different man. "You think I, owe something to youuuu?" The last word was a squeal. "My hands are cleeeean! My boots are cleeeean! But they will soooon be covered in gore and ash!"

Marsh blinked quickly. "What the hell are you talking about?"

"There will be no payout. No moneeee! I work for the great, the revered one and only, Ramses, and they call meeee the Bombmaker. But today I will be the initiator. I will give it life!"

Marsh waited for the inevitable squeal at the end but this time it didn't come. Gator had clearly allowed a splurge of power to turn his head, and Marsh still didn't understand why these people were handling his bomb. "Guys, that is my nuke. I bought it and brought it to you. We're awaiting a nice payday. Now, be good boys and put the nuclear bomb down onto the table."

It was only when Gator punched him until the blood flowed that Marsh began to truly understand that something had gone terribly wrong here. It occurred to him that all his past deeds had led him to this point in his life, every right and wrong, every good or bad word and comment. The sum of every experience put him right in this room at this time.

"What are you going to do with that bomb?" Terror

lowered and thickened his voice as if it were being forced like cheese through a grater.

"We are going to detonate your nuke as soon as we receive word from the great Ramses."

Marsh sucked in air without breathing. "But that will kill millions."

"And so our war will have begun."

"This was about money," Marsh said. "Payback. A little fun. Making the United Donkeys of America chase their tail. This was about funding, not mass murder."

"Youuuu . . . have . . . killlled!" Gator's fanatical rant ramped up a notch.

"Well, yeah, but not many."

Gator kicked him until he curled into a motionless ball; ribs, lungs, spine and shins aching. "We only await word from Ramses. Now, someone, pass me a phone."

CHAPTER TWENTY SIX

Inside Grand Central the last pieces of Marsh's puzzle began to line up. Drake hadn't realized before, but this was all part of someone's master plan, someone they thought they'd already neutralized. An enemy they hadn't counted on was time—and the way it was fast passing nullified their thinking.

With the station declared safe and inhabited mostly by cops, Drake and his crew had chance to scrutinize the fourth demand they'd finally found duct-taped to the underside of the café's table. A series of numbers written in large type, it was impossible to figure out what they might be unless you managed to squint at the heading, which was typically written in the smallest font available.

Nuclear weapon activation codes.

Drake squinted in disbelief, again thrown off balance, and then blinked at Alicia. "Really? Why would he send us these?"

"Gamesmanship would be my guess. He's enjoying this, Drake. On the other hand they could be fake."

"Or acceleration codes," Mai added.

"Or even," Beau clouded the issue some more, "codes that might be used to start up a different kind of hidden weapon."

Drake stared at the Frenchman for a moment, wondering where he'd developed such twisted thoughts, before calling Moore. "We have the new demand," he said. "Except that instead, it appears to be a set of deactivation codes for the nuke."

"Why?" Moore rattled. "What? That doesn't make any sense. Is that what he told you?"

Drake realized how ridiculous it all sounded. "Sending now." Let the suits sort it all out.

"Good. We'll get them properly checked out."

After Drake pocketed the cell, Alicia dusted herself off and took a long look around. "We got lucky here," she said. "No casualties. And no follow up from Marsh, despite our lateness. So you think this was the last demand?"

"Not sure how it can be," Mai said. "He told us that he wants money but hasn't yet supplied a when and where."

"So at least one more," Drake said. "Maybe two. We should check weapons and load up again. Somehow, with all these mini-bombs going off around the city I think we're far from finishing this yet."

He wondered as to the purpose of the small bombs. Not to kill and not to maim. Yes, they instilled terror into society's very soul, but in light of the nuke, Julian Marsh and the cells they were taking down he couldn't help but think there might be a different agenda afoot. The sideshow bombs were distracting, aggravating. It was the few men on motorcycles hurling homemade firework bombs along Wall Street that were causing the most problems.

Alicia spied a kiosk tucked away in a far corner. "Sugar fix," she said. "Anyone for a chocolate bar?"

"Get me two Snickers," Drake sighed. "Since sixty-five grams was only for the nineties."

Alicia shook her head. "You and your bloody chocolate bars."

"What next?" Beau came over, the Frenchman easing the aches out of his body with a few stretches.

"Moore needs to step up his game," Drake said. "Get proactive. I for one am not dancing to Marsh's tune all day."

"He's stretched," Mai reminded him. "Most of his agents and the cops are securing the streets."

"I know," Drake breathed. "I bloody well know."

He also knew that there could be no better support for Moore than Hayden and Kinimaka, both with lines to the President, both having experienced most of what the world could throw their way. In this moment of relative calm he took stock, thought about their problem, and then found himself worrying about the other crew—Dahl's team.

The mad Swedish bastard's probably been kicking back with a bar of Marabou, watching Alexander Skarsgård's most naked moments.

Drake nodded his thanks to Alicia as she returned and handed him two pieces of chocolate. For a moment the team just stood there, reflecting, numbed. Trying not to think about what might happen next. Behind them the café stood like a derelict old enterprise, its windows cracked and tables turned over, its doors split and hanging from their hinges. Even now, teams were carefully combing the place for more devices.

Drake turned to Beau. "You met Marsh, didn't you? Do you believe he'll follow this thing through?"

The Frenchman made an elaborate gesture. "Um, who knows? Marsh is odd, appearing stable one moment and then insane the next. Perhaps it was all an act. Webb didn't trust him, but that is no real surprise. I feel that if Webb still had an interest in the Pythian cause then Marsh would not be allowed to even pretend to do this thing."

"It's not Marsh we have to worry about," Mai broke in excitedly. "It's . . ."

And suddenly it all made sense.

Drake caught on at the same time, realizing the name of the person she'd been about to say. His eyes locked on to hers like heat-seeking missiles but for a moment they could say nothing.

Thinking it through. Evaluating. To the terrible end.

"Fuck," Drake said. "We've been played from the very beginning."

Alicia watched them. "Normally I'd say 'get a room', but . . ."

"He could never have gained entry to this country," Mai groaned. "Not without us."

"And now," Drake said. "He's right where he wants to be."

And then the phone rang.

Drake almost dropped his chocolate in shock, so absorbed was he by the alternate line of thinking. When he looked at the screen and saw an unknown number a pyrotechnic blast of conflicting thoughts ricocheted around his head.

What to say?

This had to be Marsh calling on a new burner cell. Should he resist the urge to explain to him that he was being played, a mere dupe in the grand scheme? They wanted the cells and the nuke to remain neutral as long as possible. Give everyone at least another hour, a chance to track it all down. Now though . . . now the game had changed.

What to do?

"Marsh?" he answered on the fourth ring.

A stranger's voice addressed him. "Noooo! This is Gatorrrr!"

Drake removed the phone from his ear, the squeal, the timbre rising at the end of each word, insulting his ear drums.

"Who is this? Where's Marsh?"

"I said—Gatorrrr! The fooool is crawling now. Where he should beeee. But I have one more demand for youuuu. One more, and then the bomb will either explode or it won't. It's up to youuuu!"

"Fuck me." Drake was having trouble focusing down on the words due to the random screeching. "You need to calm down a bit, pal."

"Run, rabbit, run, run, run. Go find the police precinct on 3rd and 51st and see what pieces of meat we have left for youuuu. You will understand the final demand when you get there."

Drake frowned, searching his memory. Something very familiar about that address . . .

But the voice again shattered his train of thought. "Now runnnn! Runnnn! Rabbit run and don't look back! It willll detonate in one minute or one hourrrr! And then our war will beginnn!"

"Marsh wanted a ransom only. The money is yours for the bomb."

"We do not neeeed your moneyyyy! You think there are not organizations—even your own organizations— who help us? You think there are no rich men who help us? You think there are no cabals out there secretly funding our cause? Ha ha, ha ha ha!"

Drake wanted to reach down the received and wring the madman's neck, but since he couldn't accomplish that—yet—he did the next best thing.

Killed the call.

And finally his brain processed every bit of information. The others already knew. Their faces were white with fear, their bodies wound tight with tension.

"It's our precinct isn't it?" Drake said. "Where Hayden, Kinimaka and Moore are right now."

"And Ramses," Mai said.

If the bomb had exploded at that very moment, the team could not have run any faster.

CHAPTER TWENTY SEVEN

Hayden studied the monitors. With most of the station emptied and even agents personally attached to Moore sent into the streets to help, the local hub for Homeland Security felt stretched beyond the absolute limit. The unfolding events across the city had taken precedence over the reunion between Ramses and Price for now, but Hayden did note the lack of contact between the two, and wondered if there was actually nothing for either of them to say. Ramses was the informed one, the man with all the answers. Price was just another dollar-chasing dupe.

Kinimaka helped man the monitors. Hayden went over what had transpired previously between them, where the Hawaiian had advised against forcing information out of both men, and now questioned her reactions.

Was she right? Was he being pathetic?

Something to think through later.

Images flashed before her, all miniaturized upon dozens of square screens, in black-and-white and color vision, scenes of fender-benders and fires, flashing ambulances and terrified crowds. The panic among New Yorkers was being kept to an absolute minimum; although the events of 9-11 were still very much a fresh horror in their thoughts and influenced every decision. For so many people who had a 9-11 survival story, from those who didn't go into work that day to those who were late or running errands, the dread was never far removed from their thoughts. Tourists bolted in terror, often toward the next jolt of surprise. Police began to clear the streets in earnest, brooking no objections from the ever-testy driving locals.

Hayden checked the time . . . barely 11 a.m. It felt later. The rest of the team were on her mind, the pit of her stomach rolling in acid for fear that they might lose their lives today. *Why the hell do we keep doing this? Day after day, week after week? The odds are less favorable every time we fight.*

And Dahl in particular; how did the man stay at it? With a wife and two children the man must have a work ethic the size of Mount Everest. Her respect for a soldier had never been higher.

Kinimaka tapped one of the monitors. "Could be bad."

Hayden stared. "Is that . . . oh shit."

Stunned, she watched as Ramses burst into action, running over to Price and head-butting the man to the ground. The terrorist prince then stood over the struggling body and began to kick it mercilessly, each blow procuring an agonized scream. Hayden hesitated once more and then saw the pool of blood starting to spread across the floor.

"I'm going down."

"I'll come too." Kinimaka started to rise but Hayden waved him back down.

"No. You're needed here."

Ignoring the stare she raced back down into the basement, beckoned the two guards stationed in the corridor, and opened the outer door to Ramses' cell. Together, they burst in, guns drawn.

Ramses' left foot smashed into Price's cheek, breaking bone.

"Stop!" Hayden shouted in anger. "You're killing him."

"You do not care," Ramses let fly again, shattering Price's jaw. "Why should I? You make me share a cell with this filth. You want us to talk? Well, this is how my iron will is carried out. Perhaps now you will learn."

Hayden ran to the bars, fitting the key to the lock. Ramses supported himself and then started stamping down upon Price's skull and shoulders, as if searching for vulnerabilities and enjoying himself in the process. Price had stopped screaming by now and could only emit low groans.

Hayden flung the door wide, backed up by the two guards. She attacked without ceremony, pistol whipping Ramses behind the ear and shoving him away from Robert Price. She then fell to her knees beside the whimpering man.

"You alive?" She certainly didn't want to appear too concerned. Men like him saw concern as a weakness to be exploited.

"Does that hurt?" She pressed against Price's ribs.

The squeal told her that "yes, it did".

"All right, all right, quit the mewling. Turn over, and let me see you."

Price struggled to roll over, but when he did Hayden winced at the mask of blood, broken teeth and shredded lips. She saw an ear leaking crimson and an eye swollen so badly it might never work again. Against her better wishes, she grimaced.

"Shit."

She headed for Ramses. "Man, I don't even have to ask if you're crazy, do I? Only a madman would do the things you do. Reason? Motive? Goal? I doubt it even crossed your fucked up mind."

She raised the Glock, not actually fully prepared to take the shot. The guards at her side covered Ramses in case he came at her.

"Shoot," Ramses said. "Save yourself a world full of pain."

"If this were your country, your house, you would kill me right now, wouldn't you? You would finish all this."

"No. Where is the pleasure in such a quick kill? First I would destroy your dignity by stripping you and binding your limbs. Then I would break your will by random method, whatever felt right at the time. Then I would devise a way to kill you and bring you back, again and again, finally relenting when, for the one-hundredth occasion, you have begged me to end your life."

Hayden stared, seeing the truth of it in Ramses' eyes and unable to prevent a shudder. Here was a figure who would think nothing of detonating a nuclear bomb in New York City. Her attention was so rapt upon Ramses, as was her guards', that they didn't react to the shambling steps and ragged breaths stealing up behind them.

Ramses eyes flickered. Hayden knew they'd been tricked. She turned, but not fast enough. Price might be the Secretary of Defense but he had also enjoyed a distinguished military career and now brought what he remembered of it to bear. He slammed both hands down onto one of the guard's outstretched arms, sending his pistol rattling to the floor, and then buried a fist into the man's gut, bending him double. As he did this he fell, gambling that Hayden and the other guard wouldn't shoot him, wagering on his position in more ways than one, and fell onto the gun.

And under his armpit he fired, the bullet taking the dazed guard through one eye. Hayden pushed aside the emotion and turned her Glock onto Price, but Ramses charged her like a bull riding a tractor, the full force of his frame paralyzing, slamming her back off her heels. Ramses and Hayden staggered clear across the cell, leaving Price a clear shot at the second guard.

He took it, using the confusion to his favor. The second guard died before the echo of the bullet that killed him. His body struck the ground at Price's feet, watched over by the Secretary's one functioning eye. Hayden struggled out from under Ramses' great bulk, still holding her Glock, wild-eyed, lining up Price in her sights.

"Why?"

"I'm happy to die," Price said miserably. "I want to die."

"To help save this piece of shit?" She clambered across the floor, kicking out.

"I have one more play left," Ramses murmured.

Hayden felt the ground shaking beneath her, the basement walls juddering and discharging puffs of mortar. The very cell bars started to shake. Resetting her hands and knees she steadied herself and looked up and down, left and right. Hayden glared at the lights as they flickered again and again.

Now what? What the hell is this . . .

But she already knew.

The precinct was under ground assault.

CHAPTER TWENTY EIGHT

Hayden gasped as the walls continued to shake. Ramses tried to stand but the room swayed all around him. The terrorist fell to his knees. Price watched in awe as the very angle of the room shifted, joints relocated and rejigged, inclines and slopes distorted by the second. Hayden escaped a falling chunk of mortar as part of the ceiling collapsed. Wires and ducting swung down from the roof, swaying like multi-colored pendulums.

Hayden went for the cell door, but Ramses had retained enough gumption to block her way. It was a moment before she realized she still held the Glock, and by then more of the ceiling was collapsing and the very bars themselves were bending inward, close to shattering.

"I think . . . you've overdone it," Price panted.

"The whole goddamn place is coming down," Hayden shouted into Ramses' face.

"Not yet."

The terrorist rose and lunged toward the far wall, clouds of mortar and chunks of concrete and plaster drifting and dropping down all around him. The outer door buckled and then burst open. Hayden grabbed a bar and hauled herself up and after the madman, Price shambling along behind. They had people up top. Ramses could only get so far.

With that thought Hayden searched for her phone but barely had time to keep up with Ramses. The man was fast, tough and ruthless. He stomped up the stairs, brushing aside the challenge of one cop and hurling him head-first at Hayden. She caught the guy, steadied him, and by then Ramses was pushing through the upper door.

Hayden pounded up in hot pursuit. The upper door stood wide open, its glass cracked, its jambs splintered. Of the monitor-room she could only see Moore at first, picking himself up off the floor and reaching out to correct some of the skewed-up screens. Others had been jarred from their moorings, coming off the wall and breaking as they landed. Kinimaka now rose with a screen falling from his shoulders, glass and plastic stuck in his hair. Two other agents in the room were pulling themselves together.

"What were we hit with?" Moore raced out of the room, spying Hayden.

"Where the hell is Ramses?" she yelled. "Didn't you see him?"

Moore gaped. "He's supposed to be in the cell block."

Kinimaka brushed glass and other rubble from his shoulders. "I was watching . . . then all hell broke loose."

Hayden cursed out loud, spying the stairs to her left and then the balcony ahead that overlooked the precinct's main office area. There was no way out of the building other than to cross it. She ran toward the rail, grabbed hold, and studied the room below. The staff had been thinned out, as the terrorists had planned, but some workstations were occupied along the ground floor. Both men and women were picking their belongings up, but most were headed toward the main entrance with guns drawn as if expecting an assault. No way was Ramses among them.

Where then?

Waiting. Watching. This wasn't . . .

"It's not over!" she yelled. "Come away from the windows!"

Too late. The blitz began with a colossal explosion; the front windows imploded and part of the wall collapsed. Hayden's entire viewpoint shifted, the roofline falling down. Rubble blasted across the station as the cops fell. Some climbed to their knees or crawled away. Others were hurt or discovered they were trapped. An RPG sizzled through the broken façade and impacted with the station desk, sending gouts of flame, smoke and wreckage fragments through the nearby area. Next, Hayden saw running legs as many masked men appeared, all with guns strapped to their shoulders. Ranging around they took aim at anything that moved and then, after careful contemplation, opened fire. Hayden, Kinimaka and Moore instantly fired back.

Bullets crisscrossed the demolished station. Hayden counted eleven men below before the wooden balcony that protected her began to get ripped to shreds. Rounds were passing through. Splinters and shards were fragmenting off, becoming dangerous slivers. Hayden fell back onto her behind and then rolled. Her vest caught two minor impacts, not bullets, and an intense pain in her lower calf told her that a wooden spike had struck unprotected flesh. Kinimaka also gasped and Moore rose to shrug off his jacket and remove shavings from his shoulder.

Hayden crawled back to the balcony. Through gaps she watched the assault team advance and heard guttural grunts as they called out for their leader. Ramses ran like a hunting lion, passing beyond Hayden's field of vision in less than a second. She squeezed a shot off but already knew the bullet wouldn't come close.

"Fuck!"

Hayden rose, glared at Kinimaka and started the sprint for the staircase. They couldn't let the terrorist prince escape. On his word, the bomb would be detonated. Hayden had a feeling he wouldn't wait long.

"Go, go!" she howled at Mano. "We have to get Ramses back now!"

CHAPTER TWENTY NINE

The intersection right outside the precinct was normally bustling with people, the crossing crammed with pedestrians and the roads rumbling to the constant cadence of passing cars. Tall, many-windowed buildings usually rebounded the sounds of honking horns and laughter between them, an upsurge of human interaction, but the scene was very different today.

Smoke swirled across the road and billowed toward the sky. Window fragments littered the sidewalks. Hushed voices whispered around the hub as the shell-shocked and the injured picked themselves up or emerged from hiding. In the near-distance, sirens shrieked. The side of their building that fronted 3rd Avenue looked like a giant mouse had mistaken it for a lump of gray cheese and taken enormous nibbles out of it.

Hayden registered little of this, jogging out of the station and then slowing as she cast around for the escapees. Dead ahead, loping down 51st, they were the only people running—eleven men clad in black and the unmistakable Ramses—towering above the rest. Hayden raced across the rubble-strewn intersection, amazed at the stillness that surrounded her, the clamor of quiet, and the swelling clouds of dust that sought to blind her. Above, in patches between the roofs of the office buildings—the straight columns of concrete marking a perpendicular path like lines on a grid—the morning sunlight struggled to compete. The sun rarely hit the streets before midday, it would reflect off the windows for a while early on and burnish only the cross-streets, until it rose overhead and could find a path down between buildings.

Kinimaka, the faithful old dog, hurried along at her side. "That's twelve of them," he said. "Moore is following our position. We follow them until we get backup, agreed?"

"Ramses," she said. "Is our priority. We get him back at all costs."

"Hayden," Kinimaka barely missed colliding with a parked van. "You're not thinking this through. Ramses planned everything. And even if he didn't—even if his whereabouts was somehow leaked to the fifth cell—it doesn't matter now. It's the bomb we have to find."

"Another reason to nab Ramses."

"He will never tell us," Kinimaka said. "But maybe one of his disciples will."

"The longer we can keep Ramses off-balance," Hayden said. "The better chance this city has of making it through all this."

They raced along the sidewalk, keeping to the few shadows offered by the high-rises, and trying to stay quiet. Ramses was at the center of his pack, issuing orders, and Hayden remembered now that, back at the bazaar, he used to call these men his "legionnaires". Every single one was lethal and true to the cause, many steps above the regular mercs. At first, the twelve men hurried without much thought, gaining a little distance between themselves and the precinct, but after a minute they started to slow and two cast around to check for pursuers.

Hayden opened fire, the Glock barking angrily. One man fell and the others spun, shooting back. The two ex-CIA agents ducked behind a concrete planter, staying low. Hayden peered around its circular edge, unwilling to lose sight of her enemy. Ramses was down low, shielded by his men. Robert Price, she now saw, was being left to fend for himself and barely able to keep up, but still doing well for a battered, aging man. Her concentration switched back to Ramses.

"He's right there, Mano. Let's finish this. You think they'll still detonate if he's dead?"

"Shit, I dunno. Taking him alive would work better. Maybe we could ransom him."

"Yeah, well, we gotta get close enough first."

The cell took off again, this time covering their escape. Hayden ducked from planter to planter, chasing them along the street. Bullets whizzed between the two groups, shattering windows and impacting against parked vehicles. A series of strewn yellow cabs offered Hayden better cover, and a chance to get closer, and she didn't hesitate to take it.

"C'mon!"

She made the first cab, slipped around the side and used another that had been abandoned side-on, to cover herself as she ran to the next. Windows exploded all around her as the cell sought to pick them off, but the cover meant Ramses' new legionnaires never quite knew where they were. Four cabs later and they were forcing the runners to take cover, slowing them down.

Kinimaka's earpiece crackled. "Help is five minutes away."

But even that was uncertain.

Again, the cell ran as a compact group. Hayden gave chase, unable to safely close the gap now and also having to conserve ammo. It became obvious that the cell was also starting to worry about the possibility of backup arriving as their movements became more frantic, less careful. Hayden lined one of the rearguards up in her sights and missed only because he passed by a sculpted tree as she fired.

Pure bad luck.

"Mano," she said suddenly. "Did we lose one of them somewhere?"

"Count again."

She could only count ten figures!

He came out of nowhere, rolling stylishly out from under a parked car. His first kick was to the back of Kinimaka's knee, making the big man buckle. As he kicked out, his right hand brought a small PPK around, the size making it no less deadly. Hayden smashed Kinimaka aside, her comparatively small frame as powerful and energized as any world-class athletes, but even that could only move the big man a little.

The bullet passed between them, stunning, breath-taking, the briefest moment of sheer hell, and then the legionnaire was shifting again. Another kick connected with Hayden's knee and Mano continued his fall, slamming his chest into the same parked car their enemy had used for concealment. A grunt escaped him as he caught himself, now trying desperately to spin on his knees.

Hayden felt a stab of pain around her knee and, more importantly, a sudden lack of balance. She was more aware of the escaping Ramses and the nightmarish smorgasbord that entailed than the fighting legionnaire, and wanted with every ounce of her being to end this quickly. But the man was a fighter, a real scrapper, and clearly wanted to survive.

He fired the gun once more. Hayden was now glad she'd overbalanced because she wasn't where he'd anticipated she would be. The bullet nevertheless grazed her shoulder. Kinimaka launched himself at the gun arm, burying it beneath a mountain of brawn.

The legionnaire relinquished it instantly, seeing the futility of struggling with the Hawaiian. He then withdrew a terrifying eight inch blade and swooped at Hayden. Awkwardly, she twisted, gaining a fraction of space to avert the deadly cutting edge. Kinimaka came up with the gun but the legionnaire anticipated it and swung far faster, the knife slashing hard across the Hawaiian's chest, rendered trivial by the man's vest, but still knocking him back onto his haunches.

The exchange gave Hayden the chance she needed. Removing her gun she guessed what the legionnaire would do—spin back and throw the knife underhand— so she sidestepped as she squeezed the trigger.

Three bullets took the man's chest apart as the

knife bounced off a car door and clattered harmlessly to the floor.

"Grab his Walther," Hayden told Kinimaka. "We're gonna need every bullet."

Rising up, she saw the unmistakable group of armed men hustling along the street, several hundred yards distant. It was getting harder now—knots of people had emerged and were wandering along, heading home or checking out the damage or even standing exposed and flicking at their android devices—but the sight of Ramses' head popping up every few feet was instantly recognizable.

"Now move," she said, forcing aching, bruised limbs to work beyond their limits.

The cell vanished.

"What the—"

Kinimaka skirted a car as she vaulted over the hood.

"A large sports store," the Hawaiian panted. "They ducked inside."

"End of the line, Prince Ramses," Hayden spat the last two words with disdain. "Hurry it up, Mano. Like I said—we have to keep the bastard busy and his attention away from that nuke. Every minute, every second, counts."

CHAPTER THIRTY

Together, they passed through the still swinging front doors of the sports shop and into its vast, silent interior. Displays, shelving and clothes racks stood everywhere, along every aisle. Lighted tiles provided illumination, set up in the open-framework ceiling. Hayden stared at the reflective white floor and saw dust-smeared footprints leading into the heart of the store. Hurrying along she checked her mag and righted her vest. A face peeking out from under a clothes fixture made her flinch, but the fear etched into the features urged her to soften.

"Don't worry," she said. "Stay low and keep quiet."

She didn't have to ask for directions. Though they could follow the dirty footprints the noises ahead betrayed the positions of their targets. Price's constant groans were an added boon. Hayden brushed under a metal arm full of leggings and squeezed around a bald dummy wearing a Nike running outfit into an area reserved for gym equipment. Barbell stands, weight trays, trampolines and treadmills lined up in uniform rows. Just passing into another section were the terrorist group.

One man saw her, raised a warning, and opened fire. Hayden ran hard and at an angle, hearing a bullet zing off the metal arm of a rower only inches to her left. Kinimaka jumped aside, landing heavily on the conveyor section of a treadmill and rolling through the gap. Hayden returned the legionnaire's compliment, perforating a shelf of trainers above his head.

The man inched back as his colleagues spread out. Hayden threw a pink sports bag into the air to test their numbers, making a face when four separate shots took it down hard.

"Could be covering Ramses' escape," Kinimaka breathed.

"If ever we needed Torsten Dahl," Hayden exhaled.

"You want me to try crazy mode?"

Hayden was unable to suppress a laugh. "I think it's more of a lifestyle choice than a change of gear," she said.

"Whatever it is," Kinimaka said. "Let's be quick."

Hayden beat him to it, charging out of hiding and firing rapidly. One of the figures grunted and fell sideways, the others ducked down. Hayden stormed them, keeping obstacles in their way, but closing the gap as fast as she could. The legionnaires backed off, shooting high, and disappeared around the ceiling-height rack that sold every make and color of trainers available. Hayden and Kinimaka crouched down around the other side, pausing for a second.

"Ready?" Hayden breathed, relieving the fallen cell member of his weapon.

"Go," Kinimaka said.

As they rose, automatic machine gun fire minced the trainer rack a fraction over their heads. Bits of metal and cardboard, canvas and plastic showered them. Hayden scrambled toward the edge even as the entire structure teetered.

"Oh . . ." Kinimaka began.

"Fuck!" Hayden finished and leapt.

The entire top half of the wide rack collapsed, torn apart, and fell toward them. A huge looming wall of shelves, it discarded metal struts, cardboard boxes and heaps of new canvas shoes as it came. Kinimaka held a hand up as if to ward off the edifice and continued to move steadily, but his bulk left him lagging behind the scuttling Hayden. As she rolled clear of the descending mass, her trailing foot clipped by a metal support, Kinimaka buried his head beneath his arms and braced as it fell on top of him.

Hayden finished her roll, gun in hand, and looked back. "Mano!"

But her troubles were only just beginning.

Four legionnaires descended upon her, kicking the gun away and slamming her body with their rifle butts. Hayden covered up and then rolled some more. A rack of basketballs tipped over and sent the orange spheres spilling in all directions. Hayden glanced over her shoulder, saw moving shadows and cast around for her Glock.

A shot rang out. She heard the bullet strike something close to her head.

"Stop right there," a voice said.

Hayden froze and looked up as the shadows of Ramses' men descended upon her.

"You are with us now."

CHAPTER THIRTY ONE

Drake rushed into the ravaged precinct, Alicia at his side. The first movement they saw was from Moore as he whirled at the balcony above and drew a gun on them. Half a moment later his face flooded with relief.

"At last," he breathed. "I guess you guys got here first."

"We had a little advanced warning," Drake said. "Some clown called Gator?"

Moore looked blank and beckoned them up. "I never heard of him. Is he the leader of the fifth cell?"

"We think so, yes. He's a fucked up wazzock with a gob full'a shite, but he's in charge of that nuke now."

Moore stared open mouthed.

Alicia translated. "Gator sounds madder than Julian Marsh after ten gallons of coffee, and I'd have said that was impossible before I heard what he had to say. Now, where's Hayden and what has happened here?"

Moore laid it all out for them, commenting on the fight between Ramses and Price and then the escape. Drake shook his head at the condition of the station and the inadequate scattering of agents.

"Could he have planned this? All the way from that bloody castle in Peru? Even whilst we were scouting the bazaar?"

Mai looked skeptical. "Sounds a little farfetched even for one of your theories."

"And it doesn't matter," Alicia said. "Does it? I mean, who cares? We should stop gassing and start looking."

"For once," Mai said. "I agree with Taz. Perhaps her latest lover has actually pounded some sense into her." She flicked a nifty glance at Beau.

Drake cringed as Moore looked on, now even more wide-eyed. The Homeland agent stared at the four of them.

"Sounds like some party, guys."

Drake shrugged it aside. "Where did they go? Hayden and Kinimaka?"

Moore pointed. "51st. Followed Ramses, eleven of his followers and that prick, Price, into the smoke. I lost sight of them after only a few minutes."

Alicia gestured at the bank of screens. "Can you find them?"

"Most of the feeds are down. Screens destroyed. We'd be hard pressed finding Battery Park right now."

Drake walked up to the broken balcony rail and surveyed the station and the street outside. It was an odd world that lay before him, in conflict with the city he envisaged, rocked back on its heels at least for today. He knew only one way to help these people recover.

Keep them safe.

"Do you have any more news?" Moore was asking. "I guess you've been talking to Marsh and this Gator guy."

"Only what we told you," Alicia said. "Did you get the deactivation codes checked out?"

Moore pointed at a blinking icon that had just started flashing on one of the surviving screens. "Let's see."

Drake now returned as Beau headed over to the water cooler for a drink. Moore read the email aloud, which quickly got to the point and authenticated the deactivation codes.

"So," Moore perused. "The codes are actually kosher. I have to say that that's surprising. Do you think Marsh knew he was going to be usurped?"

"Could be any number of reasons," Drake said. "Security for himself. Brinksmanship. The simple fact is that the man is six bullets short of a full mag. If this Gator didn't sound so wappy I'd actually feel safer right now."

"Wappy?"

"Batshit crazy?" Drake tried. "I dunno. Hayden's better at talking your language than I am."

"English." Moore nodded. "Our language is English."

"If you say so. But this is a good thing, folks. Genuine deactivation codes are a good thing."

"You do realize we could have reached out for them anyway once the boffins have determined the origin of the nuke?" Beau said, returning and sipping from a plastic cup.

"Umm, yeah, but that hasn't happened yet. And for all we know they changed the codes, or added a new trigger."

Beau accepted that with a slight nod.

Drake checked his watch. They had been inside the

precinct for almost ten minutes now with no word from Hayden or Dahl. Today, ten minutes was an eternity.

"I'm calling Hayden." He plucked out his cellphone.

"Don't bother," Mai said. "Isn't that Kinimaka?"

Drake whirled to where she pointed. The unmistakable figure of Mano Kinimaka lumbered steadily along the street, bent over, clearly in pain, but jogging doggedly toward the precinct. Drake swallowed a dozen questions and instead raced straight for the man who could answer them. Once outside, the team caught Mano at the rubble-strewn intersection.

"What happened, mate?"

The Hawaiian's relief upon meeting them was tempered by some terrible heartache sitting just below the surface. "They have Hayden," he whispered. "We took three of them down, but didn't get close to Ramses or Price. And then they ambushed us at the end. Took me out of the game and, when I climbed out from under a ton of rubble, Hayden was gone."

"How do you know they got her?" Beau asked. "Perhaps she is still giving chase?"

"My arms and legs might've been impeded," Kinimaka said. "But my ears heard just fine. They disarmed her and dragged her away. The last thing they said was . . ." Kinimaka swallowed with a heavy heart, unable to go on.

Drake caught the man's stare. "We will save her. We always do."

Kinimaka winced. "Not always."

"What did they say to her?" Alicia pressed.

Kinimaka looked to the skies as if seeking the inspiration of sunshine. "They said they would give her a close look at that nuke. They said they were gonna strap it to her back."

CHAPTER THIRTY TWO

Torsten Dahl left several clean-up crews to take care of the area around Times Square and drew his team deep into the shadows offered by a narrow alley. Here, it was quiet and free of life, the perfect place to make an important phone call. He first rang Hayden but when she didn't answer he tried to contact Drake.

"Dahl here. What's the latest?"

"We're in the shit, pal—"

"Balls deep again?" Dahl interrupted. "What's new?"

"No—neck deep this time. These mad bastards broke, or were broken out, of their cells. Ramses and Price are gone. The fifth cell is—or was—twelve strong. Mano says they got three."

Dahl picked up on the inflection. "Mano says?"

"Yeah, mate. They got Hayden. They took her with them."

Dahl closed his eyes.

"But we still have a little time." Drake tried the positive side. "They wouldn't have taken her at all if they wanted to detonate immediately."

The Yorkie was right, Dahl had to admit. He listened as Drake went on to explain that Marsh had now been removed as the Prince of Darkness and replaced temporarily by one called Gator. Homeland had just managed to identify this man as an American sympathizer.

"Really?" Dahl said. "To what?"

"Pretty much to anything than can cause anarchy," Drake said. "He's a merc for hire, only this time he went super ballistic."

"I thought Ramses always kept his business 'in house'."

"Gator's a New York native. He would have been able to provide invaluable logistical knowledge for the op."

"Yeah, it makes sense." Dahl sighed and rubbed his eyes tiredly. "So what's next? Do we have a location on Hayden?"

"They ditched her cell. They must have taken at least some of her clothes because the tracker sewn into her shirt says she's under a table at the Chipotle Mexican Grill, which we're just confirming is bullshit. Surveillance cameras are working but the receivers at our end were mostly knocked out by the attack on the precinct. They're piecing together what they can. And they just don't have enough manpower. Things could go real bad from here, mate."

"Could?" Dahl repeated. "I'd say we were already past bad and heading up the street of horrific, wouldn't you?"

Drake was silent for a moment, then said, "We're hoping that they continue with the demands," he said. "Every new requirement give us more time."

Dahl didn't have to say they had made no headway so far. The fact was self-evident. Here they were depending on Homeland to discover the nuke's location, running around like forewarned Christmas turkeys, only so Moore could pinpoint the exact spot, but the whole enterprise had failed.

"All we've done is neutralize a few expendable cells," he said. "We haven't even come close to Ramses' real plan, and especially his endgame."

"Why don't you guys come down to the precinct? Might as well be together when the next lead comes in."

"Yeah, we will." Dahl waved at the rest of his team and figured out the right direction to take them towards 3rd Avenue. "Hey, how's Mano holding up?"

"Guy took a big hit from a wall of shelving. Don't ask. But he's raring to go, just waiting for somebody to give him a target."

Dahl broke into a run as they ended their call. Kenzie pulled up beside him and nodded. "Bad call?"

"Considering our position I suppose it could be worse but, yes, that was a bad call. They abducted Hayden. Took her to where the bomb is."

"Well, that's great! I mean don't all you guys have hidden trackers?"

"We do. And they threw it away along with her clothes."

"The Mossad imbed under the skin," Kenzie said softly. "Good for them, but not for me. Made me feel 'owned'."

"It would." Dahl nodded. "We all need to feel that we're in control of our own fate, and that each decision is essentially free. Not a manipulation."

"These days," Kenzie fingers flexed and then bunched into tight fists, "you manipulate me at your peril," then she gave him a breezy smile. "Except you, my friend, you can manipulate me anytime, and anywhere, you like."

Dahl looked away. There was no stopping Bridget McKenzie. The woman knew he was a married man, a father, and yet still poured on the temptation. Of course, one way or another she wouldn't be here much longer.

Problem solved.

Smyth and Lauren also jogged together, passing quiet comments. Yorgi brought up the rear, tired and speckled with debris but loping along with game determination. Dahl knew it had been his first real experience of frantic, unsystematic battle and thought he'd coped well with it. The streets flashed past and then they turned left onto 3rd Avenue, heading up toward the intersection with 51st.

It was a weird few minutes for Dahl. Some parts of the city were unaffected and although many shops remained open and people walked inside a cloud of trepidation, others were deserted, practically devoid of life. A few streets were cordoned off with SWAT vehicles and four-wheel-drive army vehicles strewn about. Some areas shrank with shame at the presence of looters. For the most part the people he saw seemed unclear as to what to do, so he added his voice to what he imagined would be the authorities' and suggested they find shelter anywhere they could.

And then they reached the precinct where Drake and the others waited and hoped and planned for the rescue of Hayden Jaye.

Only a few hours had passed since this day began. And now they searched in desperation for a way to find the nuke. Dahl knew there would be no turning back, no running away or hiding in bunkers. The SPEAR team were in this to the end. If the city did perish today it would not be for the lack of heroes trying to save it.

CHAPTER THIRTY THREE

Hayden kept her silence as Ramses directed actions and reactions, reminding his men who was boss, testing their absolute loyalty. After dragging her away from the sports store they had made her run among them along 3rd Avenue, then took a moment to locate and ditch her cellphone and tear off her bulletproof vest. Ramses seemed to have some knowledge of tracking devices and their whereabouts and instructed his men to remove her shirt. The small device was found quickly, and discarded, then the group continued their run along what seemed an entirely arbitrary route.

Hayden got the impression that it was anything but.

It took some time. The group ditched their larger weapons and black outer clothing, revealing the usual touristy uniforms beneath. They were suddenly bright, unthreatening, part of a hundred anxious crowds surfing the city's streets. Police and army patrols lined some of the routes, but the cells just diverted down one dark alley and then another until they were clear. Hayden was given a spare jacket to wear. At one point they climbed aboard pre-positioned motorcycles and took a slow drive out of the inner heart of Manhattan.

But not too far. Hayden wished with everything she had that she could get a message to someone—

anyone—now that she knew the location of the bomb. It didn't matter that they might kill her—it only mattered that these fanatics were stopped.

The bikes were wheeled part way down an alley and then the ten men—eight remaining legionnaires, Ramses and Price—followed each other through a rusted metal side door. Hayden was shoved along at their center, a spoil of war, and although she already knew her fate she tried to take in every sight, every change of direction and every whispered word she overheard.

Beyond the battered outer door, a stinking inner passage led to a concrete staircase. Here, one of the men turned to Hayden and placed his knife against her throat.

"Silence," Ramses said without turning around. "I would rather not kill you just yet."

Up they went, four floors, and then paused for only a moment outside an apartment door. When it opened the group crowded in, escaping the hallway as fast as they could. Ramses halted in the center of the room, arms outstretched.

"And here we are," he said. "At a million endings and at least one beginning. The people of this city will depart this life, never knowing that this is the start of our new path, our holy war. The—"

"Really?" A dry voice broke into the tirade. "A part of me wants to believe you, Ramses, but the other, worst, part—it thinks you're full of it."

Hayden got her first good look at Julian Marsh. The Pythian was odd looking, lopsided as if part of him had folded into the other. He wore clothing that would never match, no matter the year or the current trend. One eye was bruised, the other wide and unblinking, whilst one shoe had fallen off. To his right sat a striking brunette that Hayden didn't know, but by the way they were tangled together it was clear they were associated in more than one way.

Not an ally then.

Hayden watched Ramses react to Marsh's jibe with disdain. "Did you know?" the terrorist prince said. "That we tricked you before we even met you. Before we even knew the name of the fool that would carry our eternal fire into America's very heart. Even your own, Tyler Webb, betrayed you."

"Fuck Webb," Marsh said. "And fuck you."

Ramses turned away with a laugh. "Back to what I was saying. Even the people who work here resent this town. It is too costly, too touristy. Ordinary men and women can't afford to live here and struggle to get to work. Can you imagine the bitterness that fosters against the system and the men who continue to maintain it? There are tolls on the bridges and tunnels. You are nothing if you do not have money. Greed, greed, greed, everywhere. And it makes me sick."

Hayden stayed quiet, still calculating her next move, still watching Marsh for a reaction.

Ramses took a step away. "And Gator, my old friend. It is good to see you again."

Hayden watched as the man called Gator embraced his boss. Trying to stay small, quiet and possibly overlooked, she measured how many steps it would take to reach the door. Too many for now. *Wait, just wait.*

But how long could she afford? Despite Ramses' words she wondered if he even wanted to escape the nuclear blast. The good news was that the authorities would have the airspace sewn up so the man was going nowhere fast.

Robert Price threw himself into a chair, groaning. He asked the nearest legionnaire for a bottle of aspirin, but was pointedly ignored. Marsh narrowed his eyes at the Secretary of Defense.

"Do I know you?"

Price shrank deep into the cushion.

Hayden gauged the remainder of the room, only now setting eyes upon the dinner table that stood by the far curtained window.

Shit, is that . . . ?

It was smaller than she had imagined. The backpack was larger than the standard model, too big to fit in an airplane luggage bin, but wouldn't appear too ungainly on the back of a bigger individual.

"I sold you this, Marsh," Ramses was saying. "With the hope that you would bring it to New York. For that I will be forever grateful. Think of it as a gift when I tell you that you and your woman-friend will be allowed to feel the consuming fire. It is the best that I can offer you and far better than a knife across the throat."

Hayden committed the nuke to memory—its size, shape and backpack appearance—in case she might need it. No way was she dying here today.

Ramses then turned to his men. "Get her ready," he said. "And don't spare the American bitch one ounce of pain."

Hayden had guessed it was coming. They hadn't been able to tie her hands on the way here and now she took full advantage of it. So many things counted on her right then—the fate of a city, a nation, a major part of the civilized world. The vase to her right came in handy, its neck the perfect width for her hand and of the right weight to cause some harm. It shattered across the closest man's temple, jagged pieces flying to the floor. When he brought his hand up Hayden grappled for the gun, but seeing that it was wrapped securely around his shoulder she gave up immediately, instead using her hold on the barrel to pull him even further off balance. Guns were leveled but Hayden ignored them all. This was purely last chance saloon now . . . no more fighting for her life— more like fighting for a city's survival. And hadn't they just smuggled her in here under cover? That told her a gunshot would be frowned upon.

Gator came at her from the side, but Ramses held him back. Another interesting reveal. Gator was important to Ramses. In another instant she was swamped, unable to focus outside the arms and legs that struck at her. Deflecting one, two blows, but there was always another. Not TV villains these—politely waiting for one to get punched so another could step in. No, these surrounded and assaulted her all at once so that no matter how many she stopped and struck, two more were beating at her. Pain exploded in more places than she could count, but she used a stumble to scoop up a jagged bit of vase and slash two men around the face and arms. They fell away, bleeding. She rolled into a pair of legs, sending their owner tumbling. She attempted to throw a heavy mug at the window, thinking it might attract attention, but the damn thing fell about half a meter short.

What would Drake do?

This, she knew. Exactly this. He would fight until his very last breath. Through a forest of legs she searched for a weapon. Her eyes locked onto Marsh's and the woman's but they only clung on even tighter to one another, taking a kind of comfort in an odd companionship. Hayden kicked and spun, happy with every hard-fought scream, then found the couch at her back. Using it as a fulcrum she pushed herself to her feet.

A fist smashed into her face and stars exploded. Hayden shook her head, flicking the blood away and punched right back, making her opponent fall away. Another fist hit the side of her head and then a man tackled her about the waist, knocking her off her feet and back onto the couch. Hayden threw him over the back, using his own momentum. She was on her feet again in a second, head down, punishing ribs and necks and groins and knees with punch after punch, kick after kick.

She saw Ramses step toward them. "Eight men!" he cried. "Eight men and one little girl. Where is your pride?"

"Same place as their balls," Hayden panted as she damaged them, feeling the weariness now, the pain of multiple blows, the battle fury subsiding. It wouldn't last forever, and she had not expected to save herself.

But she never stopped trying. Never gave up. Life was an everyday battle whether it was literal or not. As the power left her punches and the energy quit her limbs, Hayden still struck out, though her blows were no longer sufficient.

The men pulled her to her feet and dragged her across the room. She felt a tiny bit of strength return and scraped her boot down a shin, extricating a squeal. Hands tightened around her muscles, forcing her toward the far window.

Ramses stood over the table that held the suitcase nuke.

"So small," he said wistfully. "So incongruous. And yet so evocative. Do you agree?"

Hayden spat blood out of her mouth. "I agree that you're the whack job of the century."

Ramses gave her a puzzled look. "You do? You do realize that is Julian Marsh and Zoe Sheers of the Pythians cuddling down there, don't you? And their leader—Webb—where is he? Off scouring the world for an ancient archaeological treasure, I believe. Off following the long-dead trail of a long-dead aristocrat. Off following his own crazy footsteps whilst the world burns. I don't come close to the whack job of the century, Miss Jaye."

And though Hayden inwardly admitted he had a point, she remained silent. At the end of the day they should all expect a padded cell.

"So what's next you wonder?" Ramses asked her, smiling. "Well, not much if I'm honest. We're all where we want to be. You are with the nuke. I am with Gator, my bomb expert. My men are by my side. The nuke? It is almost ready to—" he paused "—to become one with the world. Shall we say . . . one hour from now?"

Hayden's eyes betrayed her.

"Oh, ha ha. Now you're interested. Is that too much time for you? Ten minutes then?"

"No," Hayden gasped. "You can't. Please. There must be something you want. Something we can negotiate."

Ramses stared at her as if, against his own will, he suddenly pitied her. "The sum of all I want is in this room. The annihilation of the so-called First World."

"How do you bargain with men who only want to kill you or die trying?" Hayden said aloud. "Or stop them without resorting to bloodshed yourselves. The ultimate dilemma for the new world."

Ramses laughed. "You people are so foolish." He laughed. "The answer is 'you don't'. Kill us or bow to us. Stop us or watch us cross your borders. That is your only dilemma."

Hayden struggled once more as the men pulled away her new shirt and then positioned the bomb so that it was strapped to her front. It was Gator who came forward and unstrapped the buckle of the backpack and unlooped several wires from inside. These had to be attached to the timer mechanism, Hayden was sure. Even terrorists this crazy wouldn't risk unlooping the actual explosive devices.

She hoped.

Gator pulled at the wires and then looked to Ramses for permission to continue. The giant nodded. Men took hold of Hayden's arms and forced her forward over the table, bending her frame until the nuke pushed hard at her midriff. Then they held her in place as Gator wrapped the wires first around her back and chest and then down between her legs and finally up until they met at the bottom of her back. Hayden felt every pull of the wires, every shift of the backpack. Finally they used medium-duty straps and duct tape to ensure the nuke was stuck hard to her body and that she was wrapped around it. Hayden tested the bonds and found she could barely move.

Ramses stood back to admire Gator's handiwork. "Perfect," he said. "The American Devil secured in perfect position with the object of her country's destruction. It is a fitting shrine, just as this sinful city is for the rest of them. Now, Gator, set the timer and add enough time for us to go to the zoo."

Hayden gasped into the table, at first shocked and then nonplussed by the terrorist's words. "Please. You can't do this. You can't. We know where you are, what you plan to do. We can always find you, Ramses."

"You mean your friendsssss!" Gator squealed in her ear, making her jump and jolt the nuclear bomb. "The Englishhhhmannnn! Do not worry. You will see him again. Marsh did have some funnnn with himmmm, but we will toooo!"

Ramses bent close to her other ear. "I remember

you all from the bazaar. I believe you destroyed it, ruining my reputation for at least two years. I know you all assaulted my castle, killing my bodyguard Akatash, killing my legionnaires and leading me away in chains. To America. The land of fools. Mr. Price over there tells me you are all part of a team but more than that. You call yourselves family. Well, isn't it fitting that you are all together at the very end?"

"Fuck," Hayden breathed into the top of the backpack. "You. Asshole."

"Oh, no. it is you and your family who are well and truly fucked. Just remember—Ramses did it. And that even this is not my endgame. My failsafe is even more spectacular. But know that I will be somewhere safe, laughing, whilst America and the rest of its western cronies implodes."

He leaned over so that his body crushed both hers and the backpacks' contents. "Now it is time for your last visit to the zoo. I will allow Matt Drake the honor of finding you," he whispered. "As the bomb detonates."

Hayden heard the words, the implications in them, but found herself wondering what failsafe could be more spectacular that what he already had planned.

<u>CHAPTER THIRTY FOUR</u>

Hayden slipped and bumped around in the rear of the small truck. The legionnaires had deposited her, still strapped to the bomb, in back, at their feet as they occupied the benches on both sides. The trickiest part of the entire trip was maneuvering her out of the apartment block. The legionnaires wasted no time trying to disguise her; they shoved her where they wanted her to go and walked with guns exposed. Anyone who saw them would be killed. Luckily for them, most people seemed to be heeding warnings and staying home in front of their TVs or laptops. Ramses made sure Hayden saw the truck that pulled up at the curb alongside the dark alley, grinning all the time.

Black with SWAT markings.

Who would stop them? Question them? In time, perhaps. But that was the whole point of everything that had happened so far. The speed and execution of every part of the plan had tested America's responses beyond the limit. Reactions had been anticipated, and the real kicker was that the terrorists simply didn't care. Their only agenda was the death of a nation.

They used 57th Street to head east, avoiding patrols and cordons where they could. The snarls were there, the odd abandoned vehicle and groups of onlookers, but Gator himself was a New York native, and knew all the quieter, seemingly fruitless routes. The city's grid system helped, making it easy for the driver to return to a pre-planned route. They went slowly, carefully, knowing the Americans were still responding, still anticipating, and only a few hours into realizing that the bomb might already be there.

Even now, Hayden knew, there would be White House officials advising caution, quite unable to accept that their borders had been compromised. There would be others scrambling to engineer a profit from the situation. Still more getting the hell out of Dodge and screw the taxpayers. She knew Coburn though, and hoped his closest advisors were as dependable and savvy as he.

The journey bruised her. The legionnaires kept her steady with their feet. Sudden stops and large potholes made her nauseous. The backpack moved beneath her, its hard innards always unnerving. Hayden knew this was what Ramses wanted—her final moments to be filled with terror as the timer ticked down.

Less than half an hour passed. The roads were quiet, if not empty. Hayden couldn't tell for sure. In another novel twist to his plan Ramses ordered Gator to tie Marsh and Sheers to the bomb alongside Hayden. These two complained and fought and even began to scream, so Gator duct taped their mouths and noses, sat back until they subsided, and then gave their nostrils chance to draw in a little air. Marsh and Sheers then began to cry almost in unison. Maybe they had harbored dreams of release. Marsh squealed like a new-born and Sheers sniffed like a boy with man-flu. As a punishment for them both—and unfortunately for Hayden too—Ramses ordered them strapped naked to the nuke, which caused all kinds of problems, contortions and even more sniffling. Hayden bore it well, imagining the Lovecraftian horror they might now resemble and wondered how the hell they were going to get through the zoo.

"We'll finish inside," Gator regarded the mass critically. "Five minutes tops."

Hayden noticed the bombmaker spoke perfectly well when dealing with his boss. Maybe anxiety caused the shrill rise in his voice. Maybe excitement. She refocused as the truck pulled to a halt and the driver let the engine idle for a few minutes. Ramses exited the cab and Hayden figured they might be at the entrance to the zoo.

Last chance.

She struggled mightily, tried to rock from side to side and scrape the duct tape away from her mouth. Marsh and Sheers groaned and the legionnaires planted their boots upon her, making it hard to shift, but Hayden fought back. All it needed was an odd crash, an out-of-place rocking motion, and flags would be raised.

One of the legionnaires cursed and jumped over her, crushing her even harder to the nuke and the bed of the vehicle. She groaned into the duct tape. His arms enfolded her body, preventing all movement, and by the time Ramses returned she could not breathe.

With a gentle rev of the engine the truck started forward again. Slowly, it drove and the legionnaire removed himself. Hayden sucked in lungfuls of air, cursing her luck and the faces of all those that surrounded her. Presently, the vehicle halted and the driver turned off the engine. Silence descended as Ramses, now clad in a rudimentary SWAT uniform, stuck his head into the back.

"Target achieved," he said emotionlessly. "Wait for my signal and get ready to carry them between you."

Helpless, it was all Hayden could do to breathe as five legionnaires positioned themselves around the bizarre bundle and prepared to lift. Ramses banged on the door, the all-clear, and one man flung it open. Then the legionnaires heaved the bundle into the air, carried it out of the van and along a tree-lined path. Hayden blinked as daylight stung her eyes, and then grabbed a brief glimpse of where she was.

A wooden canopy stretched overhead, supported by frequent brick pillars, wrapped around with greenery. A well-presented and paved sun-trap it was currently deserted, as Hayden imagined was the rest of the zoo. Perhaps a few hardy tourists were taking advantage of the uncrowded sights, but Hayden doubted the zoo would be allowed to admit anyone for the next few hours. Most likely Ramses had convinced the zoo's guards that SWAT was here to ensure the area was entirely safe. They were carried along a path lined by arches and hanging greenery until a side door stopped them. Gator gained access by force, and then they were inside a high-ceilinged area composed of wooden walkways, bridges, and many trees that helped with the humid atmosphere.

"Tropical zone," Ramses nodded. "Now Gator, arm the package and set it well into the undergrowth. We don't want any early accidental sightings."

Hayden and the rest of her precarious bunch were deposited onto a wooden floor. Gator adjusted a few straps, added more duct tape for stability, and then fiddled with a roll of extra wire until he announced that the detonator was securely twined around the prisoners.

"And the rocker switch?" Ramses asked.

"Do you really want to add that?" Gator asked. "Marsh and Sheers might set it off prematurely."

Ramses gave the man a speculative nod. "You are right." He hunkered down beside the bundle, the backpack resting on the floor, Hayden tied directly on top and then Marsh and Zoe atop her. Ramses' eyes were level with Julian Marsh's head.

"We will be adding a sensitivity switch," he said softly. "A rocker device that, if you are lifted or perform any big movements, makes the bomb detonate. I advise that you remain still and await the arrival of Miss Jaye's team mates. Don't worry, it won't be long."

His words sent shivers all the way down Hayden's body. "How long?" she managed to gasp.

"The timer will be set for one hour," Ramses said. "Just enough time to allow Gator and I to reach safety. My men will remain with the bomb, a last surprise for your friends, if they manage to find you."

If?

Ramses stood up, taking a final look at the package he had had made, at the human flesh and the storm of fire beneath them, at the terrified expressions and the power he exhibited over all of them.

Hayden closed her own eyes, now unable to move, a terrible pressure crushing her chest against the ungiving bomb and making breathing beyond difficult. These might be the last moments of her life, and she could do no more as she heard Gator gloat about fitting the sensitivity switch, but she would be damned if she would spend them in the Tropical Zone of the New York Central Park Zoo. Instead she would drift away to the best times of her life, to Mano and their time in Hawaii, to the trails of Diamond Head, the surf of North Beach and the volcanic mountains of Maui. The restaurant on the active volcano. The seat above the clouds. The red dirt beyond the roads. The lamps flickering along Kapiolani and then the beach to end all beaches, foaming under the spreading red fire of dusk and hassle-free, the one true place in the world where she could cast off all the stress and the worries of living.

Hayden went there now, as the clock ticked down.

CHAPTER THIRTY FIVE

Drake waited inside the cop station, feeling entirely helpless as they hung on every tip, every sighting, every barest nugget in regards to Ramses, Hayden or the nuke. The truth was, New York was too big to scour in a matter of hours and the phones rang off the hook. Its people were too numerous and its visitors too plentiful. It might take ten minutes for the Army to reach the White House but, despite all its guards and security measures, how long would it take to search that relatively small place? Now, Drake thought, put that scenario in New York and where do you stand? It was a rare event when the security forces captured terrorists actually committing their act of atrocity. In the real world, the terrorists were chased and tracked down after the outrage.

Dahl arrived at last, looking disheveled and world-weary, the rest of the SPEAR team at his back. Kenzie inexplicably started looking around and asked where the evidence room was. Dahl just rolled his eyes at her and said, "Let her go or she'll never be satisfied." The rest of the team crowded around and heard what Drake had to say which, apart from worrying about Hayden, wasn't an awful lot.

Moore simplified matters. "People are aware of a terrorist threat to the city. We can't evacuate though we aren't stopping those trying to leave. What will happen if the bomb does go off? I don't know, but it's not for us to think about recriminations right now. Our systems are shot, but other agencies and precincts have access to other feeds. We're collating them as we speak. Most of the systems are up and running. The streets are quiet for New York, but still busy when compared to most towns. The roads too."

"But nothing so far?" Smyth asked with surprise.

Moore sighed. "My friend, we are responding to a hundred of calls per minute. We're dealing with every whacko, every prankster, and every plain scared good citizen in the city. Airspace is closed except to us. We were going to close down the Wi-Fi, the Internet, and even the phone lines, but understand we are just as likely to get a break from that avenue as we are from a street cop or an FBI agent or, more likely, a member of the public."

"Undercovers?" Dahl asked.

"No cells remain that we know of. We can only assume that the cell now protecting Ramses was recruited nationally and by a local. We don't believe our undercovers can help but they're working every angle."

"So where does that leave us?" Lauren asked. "We can't find the cell, Ramses, Price or Hayden. We haven't detected the nuke," She studied every face, still at heart a civilian brought up with syndicated shows where the puzzle pieces all lined up for the final act.

"A tip is what usually does it," Moore said. "Someone sees something and calls it in. Do y'know what they call a series of hot tips down here? Two tickets to paradise, after the old Eddie Money song."

"So we're waiting for a call?"

Drake led Lauren over to the balcony. The scene below was frantic, the few cops and agents remaining fighting off the shell shock, tracking amidst the rubble and the broken glass, answering calls and pecking away at keyboards, some with bloodied bandages wrapped around arms and heads and other with legs elevated, grimacing in pain.

"We should get down there," Lauren said. "Help them."

Drake nodded. "They're fighting a losing battle and this isn't even the hub anymore. Those guys just refused to leave. This means more to them than a trip to hospital. This is what good cops do, and the public rarely see it. Only the bad ones are dragged out by the press again and again, coloring the general opinion. I say we go help them too."

They made their way to the elevator, and then Drake turned, surprised to see the entire team at his back. "What?" he said. "I have no money."

Alicia grinned tiredly. Even Beau cracked a smile. The SPEAR team had been through so much themselves today, but still stood strong, ready for more. Drake saw bruises aplenty and other wounds that were well-hidden.

"Why don't you guys reload? And pack extra ammo. When we do finally go in to end this, we're going in hard."

"I'll handle all that," Kinimaka said. "It'll provide a distraction."

"And I will help," Yorgi said. "I find it hard to follow

even Drake's accent, so will be lost with the American ones."

Dahl laughed as he joined Drake at the elevator. "My Russian friend, you have that completely back to front."

Drake punched the Swede, adding to the bruise count, and took the elevator to the ground floor. The SPEAR team then jumped in where they could, answering fresh calls and jotting down information, talking to residents and asking questions, directing calls that had nothing to do with the emergency to other designated stations. And although they knew they were needed, and helping, it sat well with none of them simply because Hayden was still unaccounted for and Ramses remained at large. So far, he had bested them.

What other tricks did he have up his sleeve?

Drake diverted a call about a missing relative and fielded another regarding uneven paving. The switchboard remained active and Moore still held out for his tip, his ticket to paradise. But it soon became clear to Drake that time was ticking away faster than milk spilling from a split container. The one thing that kept him going was that he expected Ramses to call at least once. The man had showboated so far. Drake doubted he would press the button without at least attempting a bit more theatre.

Cops ran the station, but the team helped, seated at desks and passing messages. Dahl went off to make coffees. Drake joined him before the kettle, feeling intensely helpless and out of place as they waited for information.

"Talk about a first," Drake said. "This ever happen to you before?"

"Nope. I see how Ramses managed to stay hidden all these years though. And I guess the device is giving no radiation signature, since they haven't located it yet. The man who repackaged that bomb sure knew what he was doing. My guess—ex US military."

"Well . . . why? There are many people capable of shielding radiation."

"It's the other things too. The local knowledge. The secret team he's assembled. Mark my words, Drake old boy, they are ex-SEALS. Special Ops."

Drake poured the water as Dahl spooned in the granules. "Make it strong. Actually, do you even know what this is? Did instant make it to the North Pole yet?"

Dahl sighed. "Instant coffee is the work of the Devil. And I have never been to the North Pole."

Alicia slipped through the room's open door. "What was that? Heard something about a pole and just knew it had my name on it."

Drake couldn't hide a smile. "How you doing, Alicia?"

"Feet hurt. Head hurts. Heart hurts. Other than that I'm just fine."

"I meant—"

The call of X-Ambassadors drowned out his next words, thumping through the speaker of his cellphone. Still holding the kettle, he tucked the device under his chin.

"Hello?"

"Do you remember me?"

Drake slammed down the kettle so hard recently boiled water splashed out and across his hand. He never noticed.

"Where are you, motherfucker?"

"Now, now. Shouldn't your first question be— 'where is the nuclear weapon' or 'how long until I explode'?" Deeply amused bellows blasted down the line.

"Ramses," Drake said as he remembered to switch on the speakerphone. "Why not come straight to the point?"

"Oh, where is the fun in that? And you don't tell me what to do. I am a prince, an owner of kingdoms. I have ruled for many years and will do so for many more. Long after you are crispy. Think on that."

"So you have more hoops for us to jump through?"

"That wasn't me. That was Julian Marsh. The man's freaky, to say the least, so I tied him to your Agent Jaye."

Drake winced, snapping a glance at Dahl. "She's okay?"

"For now. Though looking a little bound and achy. She's trying oh so hard to remain perfectly still."

Foreboding crawled through Drake's stomach. "And why's that?"

"So she doesn't upset the motion sensor of course."

My God, Drake thought. "You bastard. You tied her to the bomb?"

"She is the bomb, my friend."

"Where is it?"

"We'll get to that. But since you and your friends enjoy a good run, and since you're already warmed up, I decided why not give you a chance? I hope you like riddles."

"This is crazy. *You* are crazy, toying with so many lives. Riddles? Riddle me this, asshole. Who's gonna piss on your body when I set it on fire?"

Ramses was silent for a moment, reflecting it seemed. "So the gloves are well and truly off. That is good. I do have places to go, meetings to attend, nations to sway. So listen—"

"I really hope you're there waiting," Drake interrupted, fishing quickly "When we get there."

"Sadly, no. This is where we say goodbye. As you probably know I am using you to make my escape. So, as you people say—thanks for that."

"Fu—"

"Yes, yes. Fuck me, my parents and all of my brothers. But it is you and this city that will end up fucked. And I who will continue. So time is now becoming an issue. Are you ready to beg for your chance, little Englishman?"

Drake found his professionalism, knowing this was their single option. "Tell me."

"My antiseptic will cleanse the world of the infection in the West. From rainforest to rainforest, it is part of the floor under the canopy. That is all."

Drake made a face. "That's it?"

"Yes, and since everything you do in the so-called civilized world is measured by the minute, the hour, I will set the timer at sixty minutes. A good, famous round number for you."

"How do we disarm it?" Drake hoped Marsh hadn't mentioned the deactivation codes.

"Oh shit, you don't know? Just remember this then—a nuclear bomb, particularly a suitcase nuke, is a precise, accurate and perfectly balanced mechanism. Everything is miniaturized and more accurate, as I am sure you appreciate. It will take . . . finesse."

"Finesse?"

"Finesse. Look it up."

With that Ramses killed the call, leaving the line dead. Drake bolted back to the office and shouted for the entire station to stop. His words, his tone of voice, sent heads and eyes and bodies swiveling towards him. Phones were replaced in cradles, calls ignored and conversations stopped.

Moore gauged Drakes' face, then said, "Turn off the phones."

"I have it," Drake shouted. "But we have to make some sense . . ." He reeled off the riddle word for word. "Be quick," he said. "Ramses gave us sixty minutes."

Moore leaned over the unsteady balcony, joined by Kinimaka and Yorgi. Everyone else faced him. As his words began to sink in people started to yell.

"Well, the antiseptic is the bomb. That's obvious."

"And he intends to detonate it," someone whispered. "This is no bluff."

"Rainforest to rainforest?" Mai said. "I do not understand."

Drake wound it around his head. "It's a message to us," he said. "All this began in the Amazon rainforest. We first saw him at the bazaar. But I don't see how it works for New York."

"And the rest?" Smyth said. "Part of the floor under the canopy? I don't—"

"It's another rainforest reference," Moore shouted down. "Isn't the canopy what they call the unbroken tree cover? The floor is undergrowth."

Drake was already there. "It is. But if you accept that then he's telling us that the bomb is hidden inside a rainforest. In New York," He grimaced. "Doesn't make sense."

Silence fell over the station, the kind of silence that can petrify a person to helplessness or electrify them to brilliance.

Drake had never been more aware of the passing time, each second a doom-filled toll of the Judgment Day bell.

"But New York does have a rainforest," Moore finally said. "At the Central Park Zoo. It's small, called the Tropical Zone, but it's a mini version of the real thing."

"Under the canopy?" Dahl pushed.

"Yeah, there're trees in there."

Drake hesitated one more second, painfully aware that even that might cost them many lives. "Anything else? Any other suggestions?"

Only silence and blank looks greeted his question.

"Then we're all in," he said. "No compromise. No larking about. Time to take this mythical motherfucker down. Just like we did the last one."

Kinimaka and Yorgi sprinted for the stairs.

Drake led the entire team into the fear-filled streets of New York.

CHAPTER THIRTY SIX

Following Moore's instructions the ten strong team wasted even more precious minutes diverting down a side street to commandeer a pair of police cars. The call was made by the time they got there and the cops were waiting, their efforts at clearing the streets starting to show reward. Smyth climbed behind one wheel, Dahl another, and the vehicles flicked on their sirens and flashers and tore around the corner of 3rd Avenue, burning rubber straight toward the zoo. Buildings and scared faces flashed past at forty, then fifty, miles an hour. Smyth smashed an abandoned cab aside by slamming its front end, shunting it straight. Only one police cordon stood in their way and they had already received orders to let them pass. They shot through the hastily cleared intersection approaching sixty.

Drake almost ignored a new call on his cell, thinking it might be Ramses ringing back to gloat. But then he thought: *even that could give us some clues.*

"What?" he barked tersely.

"Drake? This is President Coburn. Do you have a moment?"

The Yorkshireman started in surprise, then checked the GPS. "Four minutes, sir."

"Then listen. I know I don't have to tell you how bad this will be if that bomb is allowed to go off.

Retaliations are inevitable. And we don't even know the true nationality or political penchants of this Ramses character. One of the larger emerging problems is that this other character—Gator—has visited Russia four times this year."

Drake's mouth turned to sand. "Russia?"

"Yes. It's not decisive, but . . ."

Drake knew exactly what the pause meant. Nothing needed to be decisive in a world manipulated by news channels and social media. "If this information gets out—"

"Yes. We're looking at a high-level event."

Drake certainly didn't want to know what that meant. He did know that, presently, there were men out in the wider world, vastly powerful men, who had the means to survive a nuclear war and often imagined what it would be like if they could live in a brand new, barely populated world. Some of these men were already leaders.

"Disarm the bomb if you have to, Drake. I'm told NEST are en route but will arrive after you. And so is everyone else. Everyone. This is our new darkest hour."

"We will stop it, sir. This city will survive to see tomorrow."

As Drake ended the call, Alicia put a hand on his shoulder. "So," she said. "When Moore said this was the Tropical Zone and a mini rainforest, did he mean there would be snakes too?"

Drake covered her hand with his own. "There are always snakes, Alicia."

Mai coughed. "Some larger than others."

Smyth swung their car around a blockage, sped by a flashing ambulance with all its doors open and paramedics working on people involved in the incident, and jammed his foot on the gas pedal once more.

"Did you find what you were looking for, Mai?" Alicia said evenly and politely. "When you left the team behind?"

It had all happened so long ago now, but Drake vividly remembered Mai Kitano walking away, her head brimming with guilt at the deaths she had inadvertently caused. Out of that single incident during the search for her parents—the killing of a Yakuza money launderer—much had changed.

"My parents are now safe," Mai said. "As is Grace. I beat the clan. Chika. Dai. I found much of what I sought."

"So why did you come back?"

Drake found his eyes fixed firmly to the road, and his ears pinned firmly toward the back seat. It was an unusual time to be debating consequences and questioning decisions, but it was quite typical for Alicia, and might be their last chance to set at least something straight.

"Why did I come back?" Mai repeated lightly. "Because I care. I care for this team."

Alicia whistled. "Good answer. Is that the only reason?"

"You're asking if I came back for Drake. If I anticipated that you two would build some kind of new rapport. If I thought for one second that he'd have moved on. Even, if he might give me a second chance. Well, the answer is simple—I don't know."

"Third chance," Alicia pointed out. "If he was dumb enough to take you back again it would be your third chance."

Drake saw the approaching entrance to the zoo as he felt the rising tension in the back seat, the poignant and precarious emotions bristling. They needed a room for all this, preferably a padded one.

"Wrap it up, guys," he said. "We're here."

"This ain't done, Sprite. This Alicia is the new model. She's decided not to run into the sunset anymore. Now, we stand, we learn, and we deal with it."

"I see that and admire it," Mai said. "I do like the new you, Alicia, despite what you might think."

Drake turned away, filled with mutual respect, and at a total loss as to how this scenario might eventually play out. But it was time to file it all away now, place it on the shelf, because they were heading fast towards the new Armageddon, soldiers and saviors and heroes to the very end.

And if they were watching, perhaps playing chess, even God and the Devil would have caught their breath.

CHAPTER THIRTY SEVEN

Smyth squealed the tires around a final corner and then crushed down on the brake pedal with a heavy foot. Drake was opening the door before the vehicle stopped, and swung his legs out. Mai was already free of the back door, Alicia a step behind. Smyth nodded at the waiting cops.

"They said you needed to know the fastest way to the Tropical Zone?" One of the uniforms asked. "Well, follow that path straight down." He pointed. "It'll be on the left."

"Thanks." Smyth took a guide map and showed it to the others. Dahl came jogging up.

"We ready?"

"As we can be," Alicia said. "Aw, look," she pointed at the map. "They call the on-site gift shop a Zootique."

"Then let's roll."

Drake entered the zoo, senses attuned, expecting the worst and knowing Ramses would have more than one nasty trick up his unaffiliated sleeve. The group spread out and thinned out, already moving faster than they should and without due care, but knowing every second that passed was a new death knell. Drake took note of the signs and soon saw the Tropical Zone up ahead. As they approached, the scenery all around them started to move.

Eight men burst from cover, knives drawn as they had been ordered, bidden to make the rescuers' last battle painful and extremely bloody. Drake ducked under a swing and hurled its wielder over his back, then met the next attack head-on. Beau and Mai stepped to the fore, their combat skills essential today.

The eight attackers all wore stab vests and face masks and they fought with skill, as Drake had known they would. Ramses never picked from lower down the pile. Mai redirected a swift jab, tried to break the arm but found it wrenched away, her own balance upset. The next stab glanced off her shoulder, absorbed by her own vest, but giving her a moment's pause. Beau passed among them all, the veritable shadow of death. Ramses' legionnaires fell away or skipped aside to avoid the Frenchman.

Drake fell back against a barrier, arms upraised. The fence cracked behind him as his opponent struck with both feet off the ground. Both men tumbled away to another path, struggling as they rolled. The Englishman slammed fist after fist against the legionnaire's head, but succeeded in only hitting an arm raised up for protection. He heaved the body to where he wanted it, rose to his knees and pounded down. A knife slunk up and jabbed at his ribs, still painful despite the protection. Drake doubled down on the attack.

The melee near to the entrance of the Tropical Zone intensified. Mai and Beau found their opponents' faces. Blood splashed across the group. Legionnaires fell with broken limbs and concussions, and the main offender was Mano Kinimaka. The huge Hawaiian bulldozed his attackers as if he was trying to challenge the very waves, smash them apart. If a legionnaire came into his path Kinimaka struck without mercy, a superhuman linebacker, an indestructible plow. His path was entirely errant, so both Alicia and Smyth found themselves diving out of his way. Legionnaires landed beside them, groaning, but were easy to finish.

Dahl traded hand-to-hand blows with something of an expert. Knife thrusts came in hard and fast, low then high, then to the chest and face; the Swede blocking them all with lightning reflexes and hard-earned skill. His opponent didn't let up, clinical in his execution, quickly sensing he had met an equal and needed to change it up.

Dahl sidestepped as the legionnaire introduced feet and elbows as follow ups to the knife attacks. The first elbow caught him across the temple, raising his awareness and helping to anticipate the myriad assaults. He fell to one knee, punching under an arm straight to the pit and the nerve cluster there, making the legionnaire drop his blade in agony. In the end though it was the brawling Kinimaka who smashed the fighter off his feet, pure charging muscle breaking bone and tearing tendons. Mano sported blackening bruises along his jawline and cheekbones and ran with a limp, but nothing could stop him. Dahl imagined he'd smash right through the wall of the building like a Hawaiian Hulk if the door was locked.

Kenzie found it simpler to dart around the edges of the fray, damaging those she could and bemoaning the fact that she still didn't have her katana. Dahl knew she possessed a learned, special skill and could have assailed one legionnaire after another, each a one-thrust kill, saving the team precious time. But this day was almost done.

One way or another.

Drake found his fist flurry deflected. He fell to the side as the legionnaire caught his wrist and twisted. Pain warped his features. He rolled with the abnormal bend, relieved the pressure, and found himself face to face with his assailant.

"Why?" he asked.

"Just here to slow you down," the legionnaire smirked. "Tick tock. Tick tock."

Drake pushed hard, now on his feet. "You'll die too."

"We all die, fool."

Faced with such fanaticism, Drake struck without an ounce of mercy, breaking the man's nose and jaw, his ribs too. These people knew exactly what they were doing, and still they struggled on. Not a man among them deserved to draw another breath.

Gasping, the legionnaire thrust his knife at Drake. The Yorkshireman caught it, twisted it clear, and reversed it so that it sat up to the hilt in the other man's skull. Before the body hit the grass Drake joined the main melee.

It was a bizarre and crazy battle. Blow upon blow and defense after defense, endless pivoting for position. Blood wiped from the eyes, elbow and knuckle collisions shaken off in mid-skirmish and even one dislocated shoulder slammed back into place using Smyth's own bulk. It was raw, as real as anything ever got.

And then Kinimaka ranged around it all, slamming, barging, destroying where he could. At least three of the downed, broken, legionnaires were his doing. Beau took care of two more and then Mai and Alicia finished the last together. As he fell they came face to face, fists raised, battle rage and blood lust flashing between them, catching fire like lasers from their eyes, but it was Beau who split them apart.

"The bomb," he said.

And then, suddenly, every single face turned to Drake.

"How long do we have left?" Dahl asked.

Drake didn't even know. The battle had taken every scrap of concentration. He looked down now, dreading what he would see, pulling back his sleeve and checking his watch.

"We haven't even seen the bomb yet," Kenzie said.

"Fifteen minutes," Drake said.

And then the shots rang out.

CHAPTER THIRTY EIGHT

Kenzie felt the impact like a missile strike. It knocked her off her feet, hammered her lungs, and momentarily tore all consciousness from her mind. Drake saw the bullet strike and dropped to his knees, breaking the inevitable fall. She had never seen it coming, but then neither had anyone else. Smyth had taken a hit too. Luckily, both bullets struck vests.

Reacting fastest, still with the words "fifteen minutes" bombarding his brain, was Torsten Dahl. As the two legionnaires rose from the ground, bullets rapidly fired and now taking better aim, he charged them, arms out, roaring like a train carrying lost souls from the blood-coated depths of Hell. They hesitated in surprise, and then the Swede battered them, one with each arm, and propelled them both backwards into the side of a wooden hut.

The structure shattered apart around the men, planks of wood breaking, splintering and tumbling through the air. The men fell on their backs among its contents, which proved to be most useful to the mad Swede.

It had been a workman's shed, a place full of tools. As the legionnaires struggled to pick up their guns, one groaning and the other spitting teeth, Dahl lifted a well-used sledgehammer. The fallen men saw him coming out of the corner of their eyes and froze, disbelief unmanning them.

Beau came alongside him, saw their reaction. "End them. Remember what they are."

Kinimaka paused too, chaffing at the bit as if he wanted to stomp them into dust. "They shot Kenzie. And Smyth."

"I know," Dahl said, dropping the sledgehammer and leaning on its handle. "I know that."

Both men saw the pause as a sign of weakness and went for their guns. Dahl launched himself through the air, raising the sledgehammer at the same time, and brought it down as his body descended. One blow smashed a legionnaire in the center of the forehead, and he still had strength and skill enough to turn, lift the shaft and pulverize the temple of the other man. When he was done he rose to his knees, gritting his teeth, and threw the sledgehammer over his shoulder.

Another legionnaire then sat up, groaning, head canted to the side as if in agony, and raised a pistol held between shaking hands. In that split second it was Kenzie who was fastest to react and put herself at great personal risk. Without pause she shrugged off the previous bruises, blocked the man's sights and rushed at him. The gun she held in her hand launched like a brick, end over end so that it impacted with the center of his face. He fired as he fell backwards, the shot passing overhead. When she reached him Kenzie retrieved her own weapon, but not before emptying his into his chest.

"How long?" Dahl breathed as he stormed toward the door that led to the Tropical Zone.

Drake raced past.

"Seven minutes."

That's not long enough to disarm an unfamiliar nuke.

CHAPTER THIRTY NINE

Six minutes.

Drake rushed into the Tropical Zone, shouting until his throat hurt, desperate to get a fix on the bomb. The low cry that answered did not come from Hayden, but he followed it as best he could. Veins pounded all along his forehead. Tension curled his hands into fists. As the entire team entered the building, faced with winding wooden walkways and a tree-lined habitat, they spread out to take advantage of their numbers.

"Fuck!" Kinimaka cried, stress almost destroying him now. "Hayden!"

Another muffled cry. Drake spread his arms in utter frustration, unable to pinpoint the exact location. Seconds ticked by. A brightly colored parrot bombarded them, making Alicia take a step back. Drake couldn't help but check his watch again.

Five minutes.

The White House would now be exuding such a flood of anxiety it would wash right up Capitol Hill. The approaching NEST team, the bomb squad, the cops and agents and firefighters who were aware, would be either sprinting until their legs gave out or falling to their knees, searching the skies and praying for their lives. If any world leaders had been briefed they too would be on their feet, watching the clock, and preparing a few sentences.

The world held sway.

Drake shuddered in relief on hearing a shout from Mai, then took more seconds finding its source. The team met as one, but what they found confounded all their expectations. Yorgi was standing back alongside Lauren; Beau and Kenzie tried to work it out from afar, and the rest of the team either fell to their knees or crawled alongside the mass.

Drake stared. The first thing he saw was the body of a naked woman, wrapped around with duct tape and blue wire, laying spread-eagled about two meters off the ground. Still baffled he saw that below the soles of her feet stuck another pair of feet, these belonging to a man judging by the hairy legs that were attached to them.

Hayden is the bomb, Ramses had told him.

But . . . what the hell . . .

Below the naked man he now saw boots that he recognized. Hayden, it seemed, lay at the bottom of this pile.

Then where the hell is the nuke?

Alicia raised her head from her position next to the unknown female. "Listen up. Zoe says the bomb is strapped underneath Hayden, at the bottom of this peculiarity. It is armed, has a pretty robust motion sensor and is protected by a backpack. The wires wrapped all around their bodies are attached to the bloody trigger." She shook her head. "I can't see a way through. This is the time for bright ideas, guys."

Drake stared at the bodies, the endless trail of wires, all the same blue color. His first reaction was to agree.

"Does it have a collapsing circuit?" Kinimaka asked.

"My best guess is 'no'," Dahl said. "That would be too risky, since the people attached to it might shift. The collapsing circuit—an anti-handling device—would detect Hayden's movement, assume someone would be touching the bomb, and boom."

"Don't say that." Alicia cringed.

Drake fell to his knees close to where he assumed Hayden's head was. "By the same principal then, the motion detector would be fairly loose. Again, to allow some movement from the captives."

"Yes."

His head hurt from tension overload. "We have the deactivation codes," he said.

"Which could still be fake. And worse, we have to input them on the pad attached to the trigger underneath Hayden."

"You guys had better hurry," Kenzie said softly. "We have three minutes left."

Drake rubbed his scalp furiously. This was no time to entertain doubts. He shared a look with Dahl.

What next, my friend? Have we finally come to the end of the line?

Julian Marsh spoke up. "I saw them arm it," he said. "I can disarm it. This was never supposed to happen. Money was the only objective . . . not this millions die, end of the world crap."

"Webb knew," Lauren said. "Your boss. He knew all along."

Marsh only coughed. "Just get me out of here."

Drake didn't move. To expose the bomb they would

have to turn the human pile. They didn't have time to snip off all the tape. But there was a faster way to disarm a bomb, always had been. They didn't show it on TV because it hardly made for edge-of-the-seat viewing.

You didn't cut the wire. You just pulled them all out.

But that was as risky as cutting the wrong wire. He knelt down so that his eyes were at the same level as Marsh's.

"Julian. Do you want to die?"

"No!"

"I see no other way," he breathed. "Guys, let's move them around."

Directing the team, he slowly, slowly, turned the body pile until Hayden's stomach came off the floor and the backpack was revealed. Groans escaped from Zoe and Marsh and even Hayden as they all rolled on to their sides, and Kinimaka urged all of them to remain still. Despite Zoe's claims no one knew how sensitive the motion detector actually was, although it seemed clear if it had lasted this long it wasn't set on anything near a hair-trigger. Indeed, it had to have been programmed to be all but impervious to ensure Drake would arrive before it exploded.

It was necessary to unloop the wires from Marsh's body and pick them from Zoe's extremities, a dirty job but one the team barely noticed. The ones wrapped around Hayden's frame came away easily, as they were hampered by her clothing. Now, under direction, and still held with duct tape, Marsh brought his hands up so that they passed around Hayden's right side and hovered over the backpack. The Pythian flexed his fingers.

"Pins and needles."

Mai placed her hands on the backpack, over the nuclear bomb. With deft fingers she undid the buckles and pulled the top flap away. Then, utilizing great and dexterous strength, she held the sides of the backpack and slid the bomb with its metal casing right out.

A black casing surrounded it. Mai threw the pack away and rotated the bomb very slowly, sweating now as the seconds ticked down. Hayden's eyes were bright as she stared at the bomb, and Kinimaka was already kneeling at her side, clutching a hand.

The countdown panel came into view, attached by four screws to the outside of the bomb. Blue wires snaked under it and into the heart of utter disaster. Marsh stared at the wires, four of them, tangled and wrapped together.

"Take the panel off. I need to see which one is which."

Drake bit his tongue as he eyed his watch.

Seconds left now.

Fifty nine, fifty eight . . .

Smyth fell to his knees beside them, the soldier already with his utility blade out. Taking everyone's life into his hands he took the responsibility of removing the screws. One scrape, one stubborn thread, one lack of concentration and they would either lose time or cause a terrifying detonation. Drake closed his eyes for a moment as the man worked. Behind him, Dahl breathed heavily and even Kenzie fidgeted.

As Smyth worked on the last screw, Alicia suddenly screamed. The entire group jolted, hearts in their mouths.

Drake whirled around. "What is it?"

"A snake! I saw a snake! Big yellow bastard it was."

Smyth growled angrily as he held up the plate and carefully removed the countdown panel with its flashing red clock face. "Which wire?"

They were down to thirty seven seconds.

Marsh crawled closer, eyes searching through the interwoven tangle of blue wires, seeking the point where he remembered seeing Gator arm the device.

"I don't see it! I don't fucking see it!"

"That's it," Drake threw him aside. "I'm pulling all the wires!"

"No," Dahl landed heavily at his side. "If you do that this bomb will explode."

"Then what do we do, Torsten? What do we do?"

Twenty nine . . . twenty eight . . . twenty seven . . .

CHAPTER FORTY

Drake's memory snapped to the fore. Ramses had deliberately told him that Hayden was the bomb. But what the hell did that really mean?

Looking now, he saw the three wires wrapped around her. Which one led to the trigger? Dahl pulled a piece of paper from his pocket.

"The codes," he said. "There is now no other way."

"Let Marsh try again. Ramses made a point of mentioning Hayden."

"We use the codes."

"They could be bloody fake! Their own trigger!"

Marsh was already peering at Hayden's body. Drake scrambled across and grabbed Kinimaka's attention. "Roll her."

Hayden helped as best she could, muscles and tendons no doubt screaming their agony, but receiving no relief. The clock ticked. The bomb neared fruition. And the world waited.

Marsh leaned in, following the wires around her body as Drake raised one arm, then a leg and finally unbuckled her belt where two wires crossed. When he saw the knotted pair passing again through her knees he pointed at Kinimaka. "There."

Suffering a nightmare game of Twister, Hayden watched as Marsh followed the path of every wire back to the timer.

"For sure," he said, squinting hard, one eye wide, the other closed. "It's the one on the right."

Drake glared at the suitcase nuke. Kenzie joined him and Dahl on the floor right beside it. "A specific configuration of parts and mechanisms is required to detonate this thing. It is . . . so delicate. Do we really trust the man who brought it into the country at this point?"

Drake drew the deepest breath of his life.

"No choice."

He pulled the wire.

CHAPTER FORTY ONE

Drake yanked swiftly and the wire came away in his hand, coppery end exposed. On a knife edge, everyone present leaned forward to check the countdown.

Twelve . . . eleven . . . ten . . .

"It's still armed!" Alicia cried.

Drake fell away onto his backside, stunned, still holding the wire up as if it might even now spark and kill the bomb. "It's . . . it's . . ."

"Still ticking!" Alicia wailed.

Dahl dived in, forehead-palming the Yorkshireman away. "My way," he said. "We'll be lucky if we have time now."

Eight . . .

Zoe started to cry. Marsh blubbered, apologizing for every mistake he'd ever made. Hayden and Kinimaka stared without emotion as the team worked, hands white and locked together, accepting that they could do nothing. Smyth let the utility knife fall from his hands and looked for Lauren, reaching with shaking fingers to touch hers. Yorgi sank to the ground. Drake looked at Alicia and Alicia stared at Mai, unable to tear her eyes away. Beau stood between them, his expression clear as he watched Dahl work.

The Swede tapped the deactivation codes into the panel. Each one registered with a bleep. Only seconds remained as he entered the final number.

Five . . .

Dahl hit the "enter" button and stopped breathing.

But the clock still ticked down.

Three . . . two . . . one . . .

In the final second Torsten Dahl did not despair. He did not give up and turn away to die. He had a family to go back to—a wife and two children—and nothing would stop him from keeping them safe tonight.

There was always a Plan B. Drake had taught him that.

He was ready.

Crazy mode kicked in, calculated insanity fell over him, giving him strength beyond normal. For the last hour he had been listening to one person or another flout the perfection, the accurate and exact equipment that comprised a suitcase nuke. He had been hearing how precise it all was.

Well, what if it was subjected to a bit of Dahl madness. How would that work?

As the display showed one, the Swede already had the sledgehammer in hand. He brought it down with last-gasp, final-move strength, swinging with all his might. The sledgehammer smashed into the heart of the nuclear bomb and even in that endless second he saw Drake's horror, Alicia's acceptance. And then he saw no more.

The clock ticked

Zero.

CHAPTER FORTY TWO

Time stopped for nobody, and especially at this crucial hour.

Drake saw Dahl with his body prostrate over the bomb as if he might shield his friends and the world from its terrible fire. He saw the metal casing bent, the insides dented, battered, surrounding the sledgehammer; and then he saw the countdown timer.

Stuck on zero.

"Oh fuck," he said in the most heartfelt manner possible. "Oh bloody fuck."

One by one, the team became aware. Drake breathed fresh air he'd never expected to taste again. He crawled over to Dahl and slapped the Swede's broad back. "Good lad," he said. "Hit it with a big hammer. Why didn't I think of that?"

"Being a Yorkshireman," Dahl spoke into the core of the bomb. "I wondered that too."

Drake dragged him backward. "Listen," he said. "This thing's stuck, right? Maybe broken inside. But what's to stop it starting again?"

"We are," said a voice from behind.

Drake turned to see both NEST and bomb squad teams approaching with packs and open laptops in hand. "You guys are late," he breathed.

"Yeah, man. We usually are."

Kinimaka, Yorgi and Lauren started to untangle

Hayden from the bizarre mesh she shared with Zoe Sheers and Julian Marsh. The two Pythians were covered up as much as could be but didn't seem overly bothered by their nakedness.

"I helped," Marsh said over and over. "Don't forget to tell them I helped."

Hayden ended up on her knees, rolling each limb to allow circulation to return, and rubbing areas where joint pain had accumulated. Kinimaka gave her his jacket, which she gratefully accepted.

Alicia grabbed Drake's shoulders, tears in her eyes. "We're alive!" she cried.

And then she pulled him close, lips finding his, kissing him as hard as she could. Drake pulled away at first, but then realized he was exactly where he wanted to be. He kissed her back. Her tongue flashed out and found his, and their tensions fell away.

"Now that," Smyth said, "has been a long time coming. Sorry, Mai."

"Oh hell, I miss my wife," Dahl said.

Beau stared, his face set like granite but otherwise unreadable.

Mai managed a weak smile. "If the tables were turned Alicia would be muttering something about joining in right now."

"Feel free." Alicia pulled away from Drake with a throaty chuckle. "I never kissed a movie star before."

Smyth colored at the reference to older days. "Ah, I have now accepted that Mai is not in fact the great Maggie Q. Sorry about that."

"I'm better than Maggie Q." Mai smiled.

Smyth wilted, legs buckling. Lauren reached out to steady him.

Alicia cocked her head. "Oh, wait, I have kissed a movie star. Jack something. Or was that his screen name? Ah, two in fact. Or maybe three . . ."

Kenzie moved among them. "Nice kiss," she said. "You never kissed me like that."

"That's only because you're a bitch."

"Ooh, thanks."

"Wait," Drake said. "You kissed Kenzie? When?"

"Old story," Alicia said. "Barely remember."

He made a point of catching her full attention with his eyes. "So, was that a 'glad we're alive' kiss? Or something more?"

"What do you think?" Alicia looked wary.

"I think I'd like you to do it again."

"Okay . . ."

"Later."

"Sure. Because we have work to do."

Drake looked now to Hayden, the leader of their team. "Ramses and Gator are still out there," he said. "We can't allow them to escape."

"Umm, excuse me?" one of the bomb squad guys said.

Hayden looked to Marsh and Sheers. "You two can earn extra credit if you have information."

"Ramses barely spoke to me," Sheers said. "And Gator was the biggest lunatic I ever met. I wish I knew where they were."

Drake stared at him. "Gator was the biggest lunatic—"

"Excuse me. Guys?" the NEST leader said.

Marsh glared. "Ramses is a bug," he said. "I should have stamped on him when I had the chance. All that money—gone. The power, the prestige—gone. What will I do?"

"Rot in jail I hope," Smyth said. "With a killer for company."

"Listen!" the NEST people shouted.

Hayden looked over at them, then Dahl. Drake glanced past Alicia's shoulder. The NEST team leader was on his feet and his face had turned pasty white, the color of absolute fear.

"This bomb is a dud."

"What?"

"The electrical detonators are missing. The lenses cracked, I guess possibly from the hammer. But the uranium? Although we can detect traces, which tell us that it was once here, it . . . it's missing."

"No." Drake felt his muscles tremble. "No way, you can't be telling me this. Are you saying that this bomb was a fucking fake?"

"No," the leader said, tapping at his laptop. "I'm telling you that this isn't the right bomb. It's been rendered harmless by removing all the parts that make it work. Now, it's fake. This man—Ramses—probably has the real one."

The team didn't hesitate for a second.

Hayden reached for a phone and dialed Moore's number. Drake shouted that she should call in choppers.

"How many do we need?"

"Fill the fucking skies," he said.

Without complaint, they picked their aching bodies up and made a brisk sprint for the door. Hayden spoke fast as she ran, exhibiting no physical aftereffects from her treatment. It was the mental consequences that had the power to scar her forever.

"Moore, the bomb over at Central Park is a fake. Stripped out, closed down. We think the innards and explosive detonators were removed, then inserted into another device."

Drake heard Moore's gasp from three feet away.

"And we thought the nightmare was over."

"This was Ramses' plan all along." Hayden kicked the outer door off its hinges without losing stride. "Now he detonates in his own time and escapes. Are there any choppers flying out of New York?"

"Military. Police. Special Ops, I guess."

"Start there. He has a plan, Moore, and we believe Gator's ex-Special Ops. How are the CCTV cams looking?"

"We're compiling every face, every figure. We have been for hours. If Ramses is fleeing through the city we'll pick him up."

Drake hurdled a trash can, Dahl at his side. Choppers thundered overhead, two setting down on the road outside the zoo entrance. As he looked up, Drake saw beyond the churning rotors to the office buildings where, among the white blinds, many faces pressed to the windows. Social media would be imploding today, and allowing it to carry on had yielded zero results. Truth was, it had probably hampered their efforts.

Hayden raced for the closest chopper, stopping just outside the rotor wash. "This time," she said to Moore. "Ramses won't be showboating. That was all a diversion to help him survive. This is about his reputation—the Crown Prince of Terror repairing his status and going down in history. He brings a nuclear weapon to New York, detonates it, and escapes scot free. If you let him go now, Moore, you'll never see him again. And the game will be up."

"I know that, Agent Jaye. I know that."

Drake hovered at Hayden's shoulder, listening, the remainder of the team chafing at the bit close by. Dahl was studying the nearby area, reeling off the best places for an ambush and then checking each one out with his field glasses. Odd, but at least it kept him busy. Drake nudged him.

"Where's the sledge?"

"Left it behind." Dahl did look a little unhappy. "Bloody fine weapon that."

Kenzie butted in. "I reminded him that I still don't have my favored weapon. If he gets a sledgehammer, I should get a katana."

Drake watched the Swede. "Sounds like a deal."

"Oh, come on, stop giving her ammunition. And where would I pick up a katana around here anyway?"

A voice broke in: "They're out near Staten Island, Hayden."

Drake's head whirled around so fast he winced. "What was that?"

Hayden asked Moore to repeat and then turned to the team. "We have a sighting, guys. Phoned in by a civilian, just like Moore predicted, and confirmed by camera. Move your asses!"

Head down, the team sprinted over the sidewalk and into the clear, barricaded road, jumped through the open chopper doors and buckled into their seats. Two birds rose, rotors clipping leaves off nearby trees and shooting garbage across the street. Drake removed handguns and a rifle, a military blade and Taser, checking all were in working order and fully prepped. Dahl checked the communiqués.

The pilot cleared the rooftops and then veered sharply toward the south, piling on the speed. Alicia ran through her own weapons, discarding one she had taken from a legionnaire and keeping another. Kinimaka stole glances at Hayden, which she tried to ignore, still taking in information from Moore and his agents. Beau was quiet, in a corner, as he had been since Drake and Alicia kissed. For her part Mai sat serenely, unreadable Japanese features fixed firmly on their goal. The rest of the team double checked everything, all except Kenzie who complained about the helicopter's ride, the buffeting winds, the smell of sweat and the fact that she'd ever laid eyes on the SPEAR team.

"Nobody asked you to stay with us," Alicia said quietly.

"What else would I do? Run away like a frightened church mouse?"

"So this is about proving you're brave?"

Kenzie glared. "I don't want to see Armageddon. Do you?"

"I've already seen it. Ben Affleck's surprisingly gay and Bruce Willis rocks it harder than the damn asteroid. But hell, is this you trying to tell us that you actually have a heart?"

Kenzie stared out the window.

"The archaeological-artefact-thief has a heart. Who would've known?"

"I'm just trying to get back to my business in the Middle East. Alone. Helping you fools will go a long way to doing that. Fuck your goddamn heart."

The chopper swooped above the rooftops of Manhattan as Hayden received clarification that Ramses and Gator had not left the island yet, having been sighted close to the Staten Island Ferry.

"The bits that get lost in translation could kill us all," Hayden sighed, and Drake recognized the truth in that. From the youngest schoolyard spat to a war between presidents and prime ministers—nuance was everything.

Their destination came closer as buildings flashed by. The pilot dove between two skyscrapers to maintain velocity, arrowing in on their target. Drake held on with grim purpose. The bay's rolling gray waters lay ahead. Down below they could see a cluster of landing choppers, all battling for space.

"There!" Hayden cried.

But the pilot was already plummeting, making the chopper land hard to get the primary space before a row of planters and a bus stop. Drake felt his stomach heave up through his mouth. Hayden shouted into her cell.

"Of course the terminal's closed," she said. "If Ramses is here what's he hoping to accomplish?"

"There should be some railings behind you and a line of cars parked under the trees. The cops have a woman there who was the last one to see him."

"Great. So now we—"

"Wait!" Alicia's ears caught the sounds before anyone else's. "I hear gunfire."

"Go."

Piling out, the team headed for the terminal, sprinting alongside the building. Drake spied that, behind the sweeping curve of the main entrance, a long concrete slip led out to the docking area. The shots were resounding from there, fired through an open space, not muffled as if by walls.

"Back there," he said. "It's coming from the slipway."

Choppers filled the skies behind them. A groaning body lay in their way, a policeman, but he waved them ahead, exhibiting no signs of injury. More shots exploded through the air. The team drew weapons, ran in tandem, and searched the areas ahead. Another cop knelt before them, head hanging, holding his arm.

"It's okay," he said. "Go. Just a flesh wound. We need you guys. They're . . . they're getting away."

"Not today," Hayden said and ran past.

Drake spied the end of the slipway, and the protrusions to his left, all concrete slipways used for the ferries. Waves lapped at their bases. "You hear that?" he said as more gunfire broke out. "Ramses has got himself a Squad Automatic."

Lauren was the only one who shook her head. "Which is?"

"More rounds per minute than an AK. Six to eight hundred round mag. Interchangeable barrels for when it gets too hot. Not accurate, but intimidating as hell."

"I hope the fucker melts in his hands," Alicia said.

A group of cops knelt up ahead, constantly ducking for cover as the SAW spat forth its rounds. A tracery of bullets raced overhead. Two cops returned fire, aiming down at the slipway's far end where a ferry was docked.

"Do not tell me . . ." Dahl said.

"We think he's taking a ferry right there, from one of the maintenance slips," one of the cops said. "Two guys. One trained on us, the other starting up the boat."

"He can't escape this way," Hayden protested. "It . . . it's . . . game over." Her eyes glistened with terror.

"For him," Alicia said smugly.

"No, no," Hayden whispered. "For us. We got it wrong. Ramses is literally going out with a bang. Sealing his legacy. Guys, he's gonna detonate that nuke."

"When?"

"I don't know. Best guess? He's headed for Liberty Island and the statue, and he's about to plaster it all over social media. Oh God, oh God, imagine—" she choked up. "I can't . . . just can't . . ."

Kinimaka hauled her to her feet, the big man growling with purpose. "We're not going to let this happen. We have to do something. Now."

And Drake saw the flash of the SAW about fifty feet away, the deadliness of its rounds, the one thing standing between them and Ramses, and the nuke.

"Who wants to live forever, right?"

"Nah," Alicia said quietly. "Forever would be boring as fuck."

And Dahl gave the team one final look. "I'll take lead."

In that last split-second the heroes of New York made ready; the SPEAR team and then every single cop and agent within earshot. Everyone rose to their feet, faced the spitting weapon, and made the last choice of their life.

Dahl started it. "Charge!"

CHAPTER FORTY THREE

Drake ran at the center of his friends, right where he wanted to be, gun up and firing hard. Bullets discharged from every single running gun at two thousand five hundred feet per second, multiple blasts echoing around the slipways. Windows shattered all along the ferry.

In seconds they had halved the gap, still shooting hard. The SAW user modified immediately, shocked by the ferocity of the assault. Not that he stopped firing; his bullets stitched a trail across the slipways and out to sea as he quite possibly staggered back. Drake fitted the scope to his eyes, finger on the trigger, and made out the features of the man holding the SAW.

"That's Gator," Hayden said through the comms. "Don't miss."

The SAW panned around, heading back towards them and still spitting lead. Drake imagined the barrel had to be so hot right now it was on the verge of melting, but not fast enough. A bullet caught a cop in the vest and then a second broke the arm of another. At this point their hearts were in their mouths, but they did not stop the charge or reduce the gunfire. The lower-rear sides of the ferry fell away, shattered, the open rear end so perforated it resembled a cheese grater. Gator swung the SAW hard, overcompensating. Bullets laced the spaces above their heads.

The dull note of the ferry's engine turned to a slow roar, and that changed everything. Gator jumped aboard, still firing wildly. Water started to churn from the back and the vessel lurched ahead. Drake saw they were still twenty feet from the back end, saw it turning to the left and away, and knew they would never make it in time.

Shouting, falling, he dropped to his side, skidding to a halt. Dahl dropped alongside. Hayden rolled, all this to further impair Gator's aim, but the man didn't seem to care anymore. His figure could be seen backing away, heading deeper into the ferry.

Drake signaled to Hayden and Hayden called in the choppers.

Black birds lunged to the slipway, dropping abruptly, and hovering three feet off the ground as the SPEAR team climbed aboard. At the cops' and agents' assembled salutes, a new bond formed that would never break, they saluted back as best they could, then the choppers practically leapt into the air. Pilots forced the machines to their limits, chasing the churning ferry and soon coming overhead. It was a sight Drake could never have imagined, the birds hanging like deadly black predators in the skies of New York, the famous skyline as a backdrop, preparing to take out a Staten Island Ferry.

"Hit them hard," Hayden spoke into the chopper's radio. "And fast."

Plummeting now, two choppers dove toward the

ferry's rear. Almost immediately the irrepressible Gator popped his head out of a side window and let loose a vicious salvo. His third burst smashed into the choppers' outer skin, punching through parts and glancing off others. The helicopters plunged like boulders, falling from the skies. Dahl cracked his door and returned fire, the bullets passing hopelessly wide.

"Shoots like he shags," Drake grunted. "Never hits the right target."

"Piss off." Dahl gave up trying to hit Gator and readied for the coming impact.

Three seconds later it came, only it wasn't an impact just a sudden stop. The first chopper hovered above the ferry's top deck as the second one hovered to the left side, the rest of the SPEAR team aboard. They exited fast, boots striking the deck and forming into groups. The choppers then ascended to join their brethren in the air, tracking the ferry.

Hayden faced the team for a few seconds. "We know where he is. Engine room. Let's end this right now."

They started to run, adrenalin pumping beyond measure, and then Gator clearly changed tactics on the deck below.

An RPG screamed through the air, impacting with a chopper and exploding. The bird lost control, metal ripping away in all directions, fire engulfing the black shell, and fell without power towards the ferry's top deck.

Toward the running SPEAR team.

CHAPTER FORTY FOUR

Drake heard the change in the helicopter's engine note and knew, without checking, that the machine was hurtling toward them. If that wasn't enough the extending predatorial shadow spreading across the deck drilled it home.

Run or die.

He crashed shoulder first into an outer door, ripping the whole framework away from the hinges and falling into the area beyond. Bodies dived after him, rolling, sprawling, scrambling and jostling. The chopper came down hard, rotors shearing off and metal shell disintegrating. Everything from fragments to arm-length spears chopped at the air, slicing it apart. The ferry swayed and groaned, water churning to left and right.

A fireball shot up toward the other choppers who took immediate evasive action, pure luck preventing them from colliding. Streamers of fire licked around the top deck too, starting new conflagrations, and charring paintwork and metal pillars, melting paint. A rotor bent as it smashed against a stanchion to Drake's right, bouncing to the floor with all momentum abruptly halted. Other flying missiles smashed windows and pierced framework, one terrible barb passing straight through the side of the boat and heading out to sea. Drake felt a lick of flame as the heat passed over him, looked under his shoulder and saw the entire team prone, Smyth even lying on top of Lauren. The explosion passed and they stared to rise, and then Gator took events to the level of utter madness.

Lunacy.

The next RPG came up through the boat itself, streaking out of the missile launcher and shattering decks as it flew. The explosion occurred as it breached their deck, sending more gouts of fire and deadly debris their way. Drake groaned as splinters drove into his scalp and shoulder, relieved that the pain showed him he was still alive. Taking one moment to breathe, he checked out the new environment ahead.

A jagged hole had been blown through the deck. Heaps of timber lay all around. Smoke and fire streamed through the once-enclosed middle-upper-deck.

"Way's clear," he said.

"Only to you!" Lauren almost screamed.

"Then stay," Kenzie spat as she pulled at Dahl's shoulder. "You all right, Torst?"

"Yes, yes, I'm fine. Put me down."

Drake set off at half pace, more wary than he could remember being in his entire life. The group behind him bunched together, knowing exactly where he was headed. At the last moment, as he'd expected, Dahl appeared right at his shoulder.

"We doing it, pal?"

"Damn fucking right we are."

And down they leapt, through the new hole, feet

first and eyes searching for enemies. They hit the lower deck hard, rolling, unmolested, and came up with guns leveled.

"Clear!" Drake cried.

Boots struck the hard deck at their backs.

Kenzie came last, and Drake saw, first—that she had removed her heavyweight inner jacket and, second—that she had wrapped it around the base of a three-foot long, splintered part of the chopper's rotor. Her face was smug when she turned it upon the Swede.

"Now," she said, "I have my weapon."

"Gods help us."

They stormed the vessel as one, taking the fight to Ramses and Gator. The ferry gained speed with every moment that passed. Liberty Island grew too, larger and larger on the skyline.

"Doesn't the maniac realize he won't reach the statue?" Kinimaka panted.

"Don't say it," Hayden snapped back. "Do not say it."

"Oh, yeah I get it."

"They won't sink this ferry," Dahl assured them. "The bay's not deep enough to absorb a . . . well, you know what."

On the next deck down they finally found their quarry. Gator guarded the door whilst Ramses piloted the ferry. In the mold of his already-revealed partiality to madness the bombmaker let loose the RPG he'd prepared for just such a moment. Drake couldn't help but gasp and shout for everyone to take cover, and then the missile was streaking up the center of the ferry at head height, a trail of smoke pluming behind and propelled by Gator's manic laughter.

"You like thaaaat? You catch iiiit? We already dieeee!"

Drake looked up and found Gator almost on top of him, running in the wake of the missile, carrying his rocket launcher with him. The missile itself sped through the ferry and exited the back end, exploding in mid-air. Gator swung the rocket launcher at Drake's head.

The Yorkshireman ducked as Ramses finally turned, one hand resting nonchalantly on the wheel.

"You are already too late," he said.

Drake struck up at Gator's stomach, but the man danced back, still wielding his cumbersome weapon. To be fair it held the team back for an extra moment. Nobody wanted to get planted by such a meaty stick, but the inside of the ferry was a large space and gave Dahl and the others plenty of maneuverability. Gator snarled and swung around and then ran straight to Ramses, the terrorist prince now holding a semi-automatic. Drake noted the pack strapped to Gator's back.

"You only delay the inevitable," Ramses intoned.

Spraying the inside of the ferry with one hand, he amended the course a little with the other, targeting Liberty Island.

"You were never bothered about living?" Drake said, from behind a stanchion. "The bazaar? The castle? The elaborate plan to escape? What the hell was all that?"

"Ah, the bazaar was simply a—how do you say—

'clearout' sale? A disposal of all my worldly goods. The castle—a goodbye and means to an end. You did take me straight to New York, after all. And the escape plan—yes a little elaborate I'll grant you that. But do you see now? You're already too late. The clock is ticking."

Drake didn't know exactly what Ramses meant but the implication was clear. Stepping out from cover, he sprayed the wheelhouse with bullets and ran in the wake of them, his team at his side. No more talking; this was his endgame. Ramses staggered back, blood fountaining from his shoulder. Gator screamed as rounds entered his body. Glass covered both terrorists in a jagged spray.

Drake smashed the door and then slipped, bouncing off the framework and skidding to an abrupt halt, cursing his luck. Dahl leapt over him, Kenzie at his side. The two entered the wheelhouse and raised weapons to kill. Ramses met them with all the force of a seven-foot-tall, muscle-bound madman, grinning like a feral, rabid dog; he barged and tried to fling them about.

Dahl was having none of it, standing up to the brute strength and absorbing all blows. Kenzie danced around them both, striking at Ramses' flanks like she would a dangerous wolf. The radical prince pummeled the Swede. A shoulder barge made Dahl shudder. Immensely powerful hands gripped the Swede's throat and began to squeeze. Bringing his own arms up, Dahl half-broke the hold and then took one himself; both men swaying and clutching until neither could breathe. Ramses swung Dahl around and slammed his back against a wall, but the Swede's only reaction was to crack a wider smile.

Kenzie leaped into the air, raising an elbow that she brought down with crushing strength, right onto Ramses' leaking bullet wound. Never expecting one blow to end such a struggle, she then followed up with a punch to the man's throat even as he screamed, causing his eyes to bulge.

Then Ramses, staggering, covered in blood, pulled away, retching. Dahl let him go, sensing the end. The terrorist's eyes latched onto the Swede's and there was no sign of defeat in them.

"I will take this moment as one of victory," he croaked. "And crush the heart of capitalism."

He reached out as if to touch Gator.

Dahl fired in reaction. A round slammed into Ramses' stomach, knocking him back.

Gator leapt and fell towards Ramses.

The terrorist prince managed to catch hold of the backpack strapped to Gator's falling back, his outstretched hand gripping an exposed blue wire as they both collapsed.

Kenzie shot forward, targeting the arm that held the wire with the only weapon she kept close, the best weapon she had—the crude katana. Her blade chopped down swiftly, severing Ramses' arm at the shoulder, wrenching a look of intense surprise from the terrorist.

The arm hit the floor at the same time as Gator, but the fingers still grasped the now exposed end of the blue wire.

"Failsafe," Ramses coughed. "You were right to

attack me in such a way. The clock wasn't ticking. But . . ." A spasm wracked him, blood leaking fast from abdomen, arm and left shoulder.

"It . . . is . . . now."

CHAPTER FORTY FIVE

Drake scrambled across the floor, rolling Gator onto his stomach as the madman giggled into the bloody deck. Dahl dropped beside him, pain, horror and foreboding written all over his face. The strap was buckled down, but Drake had it open in a moment and then eased the metal casing clear of the rough material.

The countdown timer faced them, its flashing red numbers as menacing and terrible as the blood that spread across the floor beneath their knees.

"Forty minutes," Hayden spoke first, her voice hushed. "Don't play with it, Drake. Defuse that thing right now."

Drake was already turning the bomb as he had the last. Kinimaka handed him an opened utility knife, which he took to the screws, moving carefully, wary of the plethora of booby traps a bombmaker like Gator could put into play. When he had the device clear of the mad terrorist he glanced up at Alicia.

"Say no more," she said, grabbed the man under the arms and dragged him away. For this kind of killer there would be no mercy.

With a steady hand, he removed the bomb's front plate. Folded blue wires came with it, stretching alarmingly.

"It's not a fucking pipe bomb," Dahl whispered. "Be careful."

Drake paused to stare at his friend. "Do you want to do this?"

"And be responsible for setting it off? Not really. No."

Drake chewed on his lower lip, hyper aware of all the factors involved. The flashing countdown was an ever present reminder of how little time they had left.

Hayden called Moore. Kinimaka called the bomb squad. Someone else called NEST. All angles were covered as Drake took a look at the device, and information rapidly flooded in.

"Pull the wires again," Dahl suggested.

"Too risky."

"I'm guessing there's no motion sensor this time judging by the way Gator was running around."

"Correct. And we can't re-employ your sledgehammer idea."

"Collapsing circuit?"

"That's the issue. They already used something new—a failsafe wire. And this bastard is the real thing. If I tamper with this it could go off."

Gator made unearthly noises from the other room as Alicia worked. It wasn't long before she stuck her head through the shattered door. "He says the bomb does have an anti-tamper switch." She shrugged. "But then I guess he would."

"No time," Dahl said. "There's no bloody time for that."

Drake glanced at the timer. Already they were down to thirty five minutes. He rocked back on his haunches. "Shit, we can't risk it. How long 'til the bomb squad get here?"

"Five minutes tops," Kinimaka said as choppers pounded down onto the ferry's decks wherever they could. Others hovered just above as first responders jumped. "But what if they can't defuse it?"

"How about throwing it into the bay?" Lauren suggested.

"Nice idea, but it's too shallow," Hayden had already asked Moore. "Contaminated water would saturate the city."

Drake rocked back and forth, contemplating madness, and then caught Dahl's eyes. The same idea was in the Swede's, he knew. Through the locked gaze they communicated directly and easily.

We can do it. It's the only way.

We'd be blind. Outcome unknown. Once started, there's no going back. We'd be taking a one-way trip.

So what the hell are you waiting for? Mount up, motherfucker.

Drake responded to the challenge in Dahl's eyes and straightened. Taking a deep breath he strapped on his rifle, holstered his guns and pulled the nuke free of the backpack. Hayden stared at him with wide eyes, a perceptive frown on her face.

"What the hell are you doing?"

"You know exactly what we're doing."

"The safe distances might not add up. For you, I mean."

"Then they won't." Drake shrugged. "But we all know there's only one way to save this city."

Drake hefted the nuke and Dahl led the way. Alicia stopped him for one more precious moment.

"You're leaving after just one kiss? Do not let this be the shortest relationship of my life."

"I'm surprise you haven't had shorter."

"I'm purposely discounting the guy I decided I liked, shagged, then got bored of in about eight minutes."

"Oh, good. Then I'll see you in a few."

Alicia held him with her eyes alone, holding the rest of her body absolutely still. "Come back soon."

Hayden pushed between Drake and Dahl, talking fast, relaying information from Moore and keeping her eyes out for first responders who might be able to help.

"They're saying the bomb has a payload of five to eight kilotons. Taking into account its bulk, weight and the speed at which it will sink . . ." She paused. "The safe depth is eighteen hundred feet . . ."

Drake listened, but headed up the nearest stairs toward the top deck. "We need the fastest chopper you've got," he told the approaching pilot. "No fucking about. No whining. Just hand us the goddamn keys."

"We don't—"

Hayden interrupted. "Yeah, eighteen hundred feet to neutralize all that radiation according to NEST command. Shit, you'll need to be eighty miles offshore."

Drake felt the bomb's metal casing slip a little through the sweat that coated his fingers. "In thirty minutes? Ain't gonna happen. What else you got?"

Hayden blanched. "Nothing, Drake. They got nothing."

"That sledgehammer's starting to look good now," Dahl commented.

Drake noticed Alicia shoot past, heading out onto the top deck and looking out to sea. What was she searching for out there?

A pilot approached, Bluetooth device flashing at the base of his helmet. "We got the fastest goddamn chopper in the Army," he drawled. "Bell SuperCobra. Two hundred miles per hour if you push her."

Drake turned to Hayden. "Will that work?"

"I think so." She did a few mental arithmetic calculations in her head. "Wait, that can't be right."

Drake clung onto the nuke, the red numbers still flashing, Dahl at his side. "Come on!"

"Eighty miles," she said, running. "Yes, you can do it. But that'll leave you only . . . three minutes to get the hell out of there. You won't escape the blast zone!"

Drake approached the SuperCobra without slowing, eyes taking in the sleek gray shape, turret mounts, three barrel cannons, rocket pods and Hellfire missile launchers.

"That'll do," he said.

"Drake," Hayden stopped him. "Even if you do drop the nuke safely the blast will destroy you."

"Then stop wasting our time," the Yorkshireman said. "Unless you or Moore or any of the other bods in your head know of another way?"

Hayden listened to the data, advice and intelligence Moore was constantly passing on. Drake felt the ferry bobbing on the rolling waters, saw the skyline of Manhattan in the near distance, even made out the ant-like scurrying of people already returning to their lives. Military vessels, speedboats and choppers sat all around, manned by many who would give their lives to save this day.

But it came down to just two.

Drake and Dahl climbed aboard the SuperCobra, receiving a crash course in its operation from the exiting pilot.

"Godspeed," he said, departing. "And good luck."

CHAPTER FORTY SIX

Drake passed the nuke to Dahl, a little smile on his face. "Figured you'd want to do the honors, mate."

The Swede hefted the bomb and climbed into the rear of the chopper. "I'm not sure I can trust you to drive in a straight line."

"It's not a car. And I do believe we already established I can drive better than you."

"Why's that? I don't remember it that way."

"I'm English. You ain't."

"And what exactly does nationality have to do with it?" Dahl slipped into a seat.

"Pedigree," Drake said. "Stewart. Hamilton. Hunt. Button. Hill. And more. The closest Sweden came to winning F1 was when Finland came first."

Dahl laughed, buckling in and setting the black metal casing along his lap, pulling the door closed. "Don't talk so loud, Drake. The bomb might be equipped with a 'bollocks' sensor."

"Then we're already fucked."

Hauling on the cyclic stick he lifted the chopper clear of the ferry after checking that the skies above were clear. Sunlight flashed behind and caught the city's million reflective surfaces, giving him a little reminder of why they were doing this. Upturned faces stared with respect from the deck below, many of them his friends and family, his team mates. Kenzie and Mai stood shoulder to shoulder, their faces expressionless, but it was the Israeli who ultimately made him smile.

She tapped her watch and mouthed: *Get a fuckin' move on.*

Alicia was nowhere to be seen, nor Beau. Drake sent the military chopper swooping low over the waves and on a straight course across the Atlantic. Winds crisscrossed their path and sunlight glimmered atop every rolling swell. Horizons hung suspended to all sides, vaults of light blue sky competing with the awe-inspiring vastness of the seas. The epic skyline at their back fell away as the minutes and seconds ticked slowly toward zero.

"Fifteen minutes," Dahl said.

Drake eyed the odometer. "Right on schedule."

"How much time will we have spare?"

"Three minutes," Drake rolled a hand. "Give or take."

"What's that in miles?"

"At two hundred miles per hour? Roughly, seven."

Dahl raised a hopeful expression. "Not bad."

"In a perfect world," Drake shrugged. "Doesn't include turn maneuvers, speeding up, shark attack. Whatever the hell else they might throw at us out there."

"This thing have an inflatable?" Dahl cast around, fingers clutched tight to the nuke.

"If it does, I don't know where." Drake watched the clock.

Twelve minutes to explosion.

"Get ready."

"Always am."

"Bet you didn't expect to be doing this when you woke up today."

"What? Dropping a nuclear bomb into the Atlantic Ocean to save New York City? Or talking to you, face to face, whilst riding a marine's chopper?"

"Well, both."

"The first part crossed my mind."

Drake shook his head, unable to hide a smile. "Of course it did. You're Torsten Dahl, the great hero."

The Swede relinquished his grip on the nuke for just one second to place a hand on Drake's shoulder. "And you're Drake, Matt Drake, the most caring person I have ever known. No matter how hard you try to hide it."

"You ready to drop that nuke?"

"Of course I am, ya daft Northern dickhead."

Drake made the chopper dive, plummeting nose first toward the gray swell. Dahl threw open the rear door, shuffling around to get the best position. A current of air gusted through the SuperCobra. Drake tightened his grip on the stick and worked the pedals, still plummeting. Dahl shifted the nuke one last time. Waves tossed and collided and sent errant spray flaring up to meet them, a white foam laced through with diamond sparkles of sunlight. Bracing every muscle, Drake finally pulled up hard, leveling the halo off and spinning his head to watch Dahl heave the metal-cased weapon of ultimate destruction out the door.

It fell toward the waves, a spinning bomb, entering the water easily because of the low altitude it had been released at, another failsafe to ensure the anti-tamper sensor remained neutral. Drake instantly gunned them away from the point of impact, skimming the waves so low they washed over his skids, wasting no time in climbing and giving the chopper less space to fall through in case of calamity.

Dahl checked his own watch.

Two minutes.

"Get your foot down."

Drake almost repeated that he wasn't actually driving a car but concentrated instead in coaxing every modicum of speed from the bird, knowing that the Swede was just venting tension. Everything was down to seconds now—the time before the nuke exploded, the miles they were distant from its blast radius, the span of their lives.

"Eighteen seconds," Dahl said.

Drake prepared for hell. "Been a pleasure, mate."

Ten . . . nine . . .

"See you soon, Yorkie."

Six . . . five . . . four . . .

"Not if I see your stupid—"

Zero.

CHAPTER FORTY SEVEN

Drake and Dahl saw nothing of the initial underwater explosion, but the enormous wall of water that erupted from the sea behind them was enough to make their hearts falter. A liquid mushroom cloud exploding thousands of feet into the air, dwarfing all else, shooting up toward the atmosphere as if striving to drown out the very sun. A spray dome surged up, the precursor to shock waves, a spherical cloud, high surface waves and a base surge that would rise to a height beyond five hundred meters.

The blast wave was unstoppable, a manmade force of nature, an energy corruption. It struck the rear of the chopper like a hammer blow, giving Drake the impression he was being pushed along by the hand of a malicious giant. Almost immediately the chopper swooped, lifted and then turned to the side. Drake's head struck metal. Dahl clung on, a rag doll being thrown around by a vicious hound.

The chopper rocked and rolled, buffeted and beaten by the endless blast, the dynamic wave. It spun again and again, its rotors slowing, its body pitching. Behind it, the immense curtain of water continued to rise, propelled by a titanic force. Drake struggled to stay conscious, abandoning all control of his destiny and just trying to hang on, remain awake and in one piece.

Time was rendered irrelevant and they might have

lurched and bucked inside that blast wave for hours, but it was only when it surged past and they found themselves in its wake, that the true toll of its devastating power became clear.

The chopper, almost upside down, plunged toward the Atlantic.

Out of control, Drake braced himself for the impact with the knowledge that, even if they did survive the crash, they had no life raft, no life vests, and no hope of rescue. Somehow retaining enough cognizance to hold on with every last ounce of strength, he watched as they plunged into the ocean.

CHAPTER FORTY EIGHT

Alicia saw Drake make the connection in his head about three seconds after her. Dahl too. The boys were slow, but she'd never tell. It was far better to hold some things in reserve. As the rest caught on and Hayden sought advice from Moore and his government cronies, Alicia took on board the fateful knowledge that the law of safe distances was going to make them all suffer badly sometime in the next half hour. As Drake worked toward appropriating a chopper, Alicia turned her eyes and her attention to something else.

A chopper would crash, she knew that, so the obvious choice of tailing him in another bird didn't made a jot of sense. But if his helicopter flew at two hundred miles an hour . . .

Alicia pulled Beau aside, explained her plan and then found a soldier who introduced them to a representative of the US Coastguard.

"What's the fastest ship you've got?"

By the time Drake lifted off, Alicia was heading below decks and jumping aboard a hastily scrambled Defender Class boat, good for over eighty miles per hour. As one of the sheepish crew attested, they had made some modifications, which may or may not have increased the boat's speed to over one hundred. When Alicia told them in just a few terse words what she wanted to do every man there insisted on staying to help.

The Defender roared away minutes later, pounding at the seas with a rigid hull, trying to narrow that gap between the inevitable detonation and their time of arrival.

As Alicia told them: "We're racing toward the nuclear explosion, boys. Hold on to yer plums."

And whether they understood or not, the crew coaxed every ounce of speed from the boat. Riding the waves, challenging them, the Defender class boat gave everything it had. Alicia clung with white knuckles and white face to railings inside the cabin, watching through the windows. A GPS charted the course of the chopper, having plotted its transponder signal. The ship's crew constantly worked out the time differences, saying they had narrowed the gap to twenty minutes then eighteen.

Seventeen.

Still too long. Alicia gripped the rail and then started when Beau seized her shoulder.

"It will work," he said. "We will save this day."

The boat raced hard, pursuing the speeding chopper, both of them bizarrely chasing an oncoming explosion that hadn't happened yet. The horizon was an ever-changing line, never straight. The crew sweated and struggled and plumbed the depths of their knowledge. The boat edged into unknown territory, engines so virile they felt alive.

When the captain turned to Alicia, she had already seen the spiraling cloud on the horizon, not too far distant, but much further away than Drake and Dahl's helicopter. The speeding Defender zipped off the top of one large surge of water, saw and struck the approaching blast wave, and broke through, shuddering every bolt that held fast its structure. The great ring of white water was visible in the distance, the spectacle stopping even Alicia's runaway mouth for a second.

But only for a second.

"Move," she breathed, conscious of Drake and Dahl now almost certainly crashing into hostile waters. "Move, move, move!"

It took another thirteen minutes to reach the crash site. Alicia was ready, life vest strapped around her body and another held in her hand. Beau was at her side with more than half a dozen crewmen, eyes searching the waters. The first debris they found was a floating piece of rotor blade, the second a full length skid. After that those parts that hadn't sunk came more frequently, passing by in a clump.

But no Drake, and no Dahl.

Alicia scanned the waves, standing in the bright sunshine but living in the darkest hell. If the fates determined that these two heroes could save New York and survive the explosion, only to be lost in the Atlantic, she was not sure she'd be able to handle that. Minutes passed. Wreckage floated by. Nobody spoke, nor moved an inch. They would remain until nightfall if need be.

The radio crackled constantly. Hayden's voice,

enquiring. Then Moore's and Smyth's on a different line. Even Kenzie spoke up. The moments passed in slow-motion turmoil, burgeoning dread. The longer it took . . .

Beau rose onto his tiptoes, catching sight of something just rising up the side of a swell. He pointed it out and voiced a question. Alicia then saw it too, an odd black mass, moving sluggishly.

"If that's a Kraken," she mostly whispered without realizing she'd even spoken. "I'm outta here."

The captain leaned the boat in that direction, helping the form gain focus. It took a few minutes and a little drifting, but as Alicia squinted she saw that it was two bodies, lashed together so that they wouldn't float apart, and tied to the still-floating pilot's seat. The battle between treading water and sinking seemed to be tilting toward the latter, so Alicia urged the Defender to hurry.

And jumped overboard.

Swimming hard, she grasped hold of the bobbing mass and heaved it around, trying to make sense of it. A face swiveled around.

"Dahl. Are you all right? Where's Drake?"

"Hanging on to my coat tails. As always."

As the current shifted Dahl around in the water a second face became visible, resting against the back of the other's jacket.

"Well, you two look bloody comfy together," Alicia mock-protested. "No wonder you didn't shout out for rescue. Shall we give you another ten minutes or so?"

Drake's shaking hand rose from the waters. "Not

even one. I think I swallowed half the bloody ocean."

"And I think we're about to go under," Dahl gasped a moment before the pilot's seat drifted away and his head disappeared below the waters.

The Coastguard boat came as close as it dared. "Are they okay?" voices hollered.

Alicia waved. "They're fine. Bastards are just messing about."

Then Drake slipped under too.

"Umm," Alicia stared. "Actually . . ."

CHAPTER FORTY NINE

In the aftermath the world adjusted, shocked by the near-miss horror of what had occurred, but sadly inured to it too. As the United States detailed back in the 1960s, it was only a matter of time before some terrorist detonated a nuclear bomb in one of the world's major cities. They had even developed a document and reaction to it—National Response Scenario Number One.

If a more wounded, bruised, sore and complaining group of people assembled to debate the consequences and gloss over the near-misses of New York, then it was never acknowledged. This team, however, SPEAR and a few others, were contacted by the President, the Director of Homeland Security, and the Mayor of New York.

Alicia was always going to complain about it. "And all I really wanted was a call from Lawrence."

"Fishburne?" Drake asked.

"Don't be silly. Jennifer, of course."

"Could she steal you away from me?"

Alicia ginned. "In a heartbeat."

"Well, it's always nice to know where you stand."

"If you like I could write you a list of principal suitors."

Drake waved a hand, still trying to come to terms with the kiss they had shared. It had happened right after a moment of great stress, a celebration of life, but it had stirred emotions, old emotions, inside him that he thought were long dead. As everything stood right now there were many other things to consider— Mai and Beau chief among them.

But life didn't decelerate just for you, he thought. Though many expected it to, and great chances mostly came along but once. To miss them usually meant a lifetime of regret, of never knowing. A chance taken was never a chance lost.

Better to try and fail than to never try at all.

Alicia was as complex as a solar system, but even that was navigable. He switched his thoughts off for a moment, still physically and mentally weak from all the exertions of the day and, indeed, the last few weeks. Around him sat his friends, enjoying a sit-down meal inside one of New York's best Italian restaurants. Agent Moore had rented the entire place out at Homeland's expense, as a thank you to the team, and locked them inside.

"No matter what happens," he said. "I don't want you people rushing off to prevent it."

Drake appreciated that.

And the team appreciated the fine food, the relaxed atmosphere, and the long break from such intense stress. The seats were plush, the room warm, the staff barely noticeable. Dahl had dressed in white shirt and black trousers, almost unrecognizable to Drake who was used to seeing him in combat gear. But then he had dressed similar, substituting the trousers for trusty Levis.

"That's not the Bond look," Dahl had pointed out.

"I'm not James Bond."

"Then stop poncing about and trying to sound more sophisticated every time Alicia walks by. She already knows you're just a Yorkshire tw—"

"I think it's time you pissed off on vacation, pal. If you can't decide where to go I'd be happy to knock you into next week." He held up a fist.

"And there's my thanks for saving your life."

"Don't remember it. And if I don't remember it, it never happened."

"Much like the time you matured."

Beau and Mai sat next to each other, the Frenchman enjoying the food and speaking when spoken to; the Japanese woman looking out of place, caught between two worlds. Drake wondered what she really wanted and where she truly belonged. In some moments he saw a fire in her that prompted her to fight for him, in others a doubt that sent her silent, introspective. Certainly, the four of them couldn't resolve anything in a day, but he saw something coming, clouding the horizon ahead.

Much like the nuclear explosion he witnessed yesterday.

Smyth and Lauren were now an item. Maybe the kiss between Drake and Alicia prompted them, or maybe the brush with annihilation. Either way, they weren't wasting another day wondering. Hayden and Kinimaka sat together, and Drake wondered if he saw more than the meter gap between them, something with more significance. It had more to do with body language than anything, but then he was mentally fizzled out and put it down to weariness.

"To tomorrow," he raised a glass, "and the next battle."

Drinks were drained and the meal continued. It was after the main course had been devoured, and most sat back draped beneath a contented drowsiness, that Kenzie made a point of speaking in front of the entire group.

"And what of me?" she asked. "Is my fate so uncertain?"

Hayden shifted, the mantle of leadership coating her once more. "Well, I'll be blunt with you, which I'm sure you'll appreciate. There is nothing I'd like better than to keep you out of a jail cell, Kenzie, but I have to say—I can't see it happening."

"I could walk away."

"I couldn't stop you," Hayden acknowledged. "And wouldn't want to. But the crimes you have committed in the Middle East—" she made a face "—at the very least upset a great many powerful people. Some of them American."

"Most likely the same men and women I procured other items for."

"A good point. But not helpful."

"Then I will join your team. Turn over a new leaf. Run alongside the blond gazelle that is Torsten Dahl. I am now yours, Hayden, if you will give me chance to work off my debt."

The SPEAR team leader blinked rapidly as she took in Kenzie's heartfelt statement. Drake choked on his water, for the second time in two days. "I never thought of Dahl as a gazelle. More a—"

"Don't say it," the Swede warned, looking slightly embarrassed.

Alicia watched the Israeli closely. "I'm not sure I want to work with this bitch."

"Oh, I will be good for you, Myles. Keep you on those toes. I could teach you how to throw a punch that actually hurts."

"I may also have to stick with you for now," Beau spoke up. "With Tyler Webb in the wind and playing Tomb Raider, I have no other place to be."

"Thanks," Drake grunted. "We'll think about it and mail you a very short letter of response."

"Good people are always welcomed to this team," Hayden told him. "So long as they play nicely with the rest of us. I'm sure Beau will be a great asset."

"Well, I for one know he has a great asset," Alicia said reflectively. "Though I'm not sure it would play nicely with the team."

Some laughed and some didn't. The night waxed and then waned and still, the soldiers who saved New York depressurized themselves among good company and good stories. The city itself celebrated with them, though the majority of its inhabitants never knew why. A sense of carnival saturated the air. In darkness, and then the rising dawn, life went on.

As a new day dawned the team drifted apart, heading back to hotel rooms and agreeing to meet that afternoon.

"Ready to fight another day?" Dahl yawned at Drake as they walked into the crisp, new morning.

"Alongside you?" Drake thought about ribbing the

Swede and then remembered all they had been through. Not just today but since the day they met.

"Always," he said.

THE END

Please read on for more information on the future of the Matt Drake world:

I hope you enjoyed this book, possibly the fastest paced novel yet and set over the shortest time. Coming soon, in early June, will be the Torsten Dahl stand-alone, *Stand Your Ground,* something very special I've been planning and plotting since late 2015. After that it will be the next Drake, possibly the landmark in the Drake series that brings the Pythians' story to a close and presents the long-promised story around Le Comte de Saint Germain. I'll also be trying to slot in Alicia 3 and Chosen 3 at some point!

First hand, release-related news, updates and giveaways can be found on my Facebook page— https://www.facebook.com/davidleadbeaternovels/ Website: www.davidleadbeater.com.

And remember:
Reviews are everything to an author and essential to the future of the Matt Drake, Alicia Myles and other series. Please consider leaving even a few lines at Amazon, it will make all the difference.

Printed in Great Britain
by Amazon